The WEDNESDAY
FLOWER MAN

D1282554

The WEDNESDAY FLOWER MAN

DIANNE WARREN

for my mother and for Rhonda

Some of the stories in this collection, or earlier versions of them, first appeared as follows: "Modern Girls" in *NeWest Review*; "The Elite Cafe" in *Saskatchewan Gold*; "Dead Rabbits" in *Dinosaur Review*; and "Sunday Rodeos" and "The Winter Road" in *Grain*.

The lines from "Famous Blue Raincoat" which appear on page vii are copyright © Leonard Cohen. Used with permission. All rights reserved.

Cover illustration: "The Handsome Waiter" by Iris Hauser, 1985.
Reproduced here courtesy of the artist.
Cover and book design by Brent Smith.
Typeset by Publication Associates (Regina) Limited.
Printed by Hignell Printing Limited.

The author would like to thank members of the Bombay Bicycle Club, and Edna Alford for her editorial advice.

The publisher gratefully acknowledges the financial assistance of the Saskatchewan Arts Board, the Canada Council, the Department of Communications, and the City of Regina in the publication of this book.

**Saskatchewan
Arts Board**

Canadian Cataloguing in Publication Data
Warren, Dianne, 1950-
  The Wednesday flower man

(McCourt fiction series ; 4)

  ISBN 0-919926-69-X (bound) — ISBN 0-919926-68-1 (pbk.)

I. Title. II. Series.

PS8595.A76W4 1987   C813'.54   C87-098077-7
PR9199.3.S33D6 1987

coteau books

Thunder Creek Publishing Co-operative Limited
Box 239, Sub #1
Moose Jaw, Saskatchewan
S6H 5V0

CONTENTS

WEAK HEARTS 1

THE WINTER ROAD 13

THE WEDNESDAY FLOWER MAN 25

SUNDAY RODEOS 41

THE ELITE CAFE 47

MODERN GIRLS 57

THE CLEARING 65

REAL FAMOUS MEN 75

GLORY DAYS 89

HOW I DIDN'T KILL WALLY
EVEN THOUGH HE DESERVES IT 101

SUKIE 113

FINE BONE CHINA 121

COME DAYLIGHT 129

DEAD RABBITS 149

MIRACLES NIGHTLY 155

I hear that you're building your house deep in the desert
Are you living for nothing now
Hope you're keeping some kind of record

> *from* "Famous Blue Raincoat" *by Leonard Cohen*

WEAK HEARTS

She was wearing a red shimmery dress and those ridiculous red dance shoes that she picked up at a garage sale. She liked them because they looked like the ones Judy Garland wore in *The Wizard of Oz*. He didn't like her in red, and besides it was a wedding and women shouldn't wear red to a wedding. Still, he knew better than to say anything. They were sitting at a table with three other couples, none of whom they knew. The woman directly across the table from him (she looked a bit familiar) was wearing a hat, a kind of fedora, tipped down over one eye. She was with a blond guy who looked like he had lots of muscles under his jacket. Alec wondered why it was all right for a woman to wear a hat at the table. A man couldn't get away with that. Not that he would want to. What's the point of wearing a hat to dinner?

Rose had not wanted to come to this wedding. She had managed to miss the ceremony simply by not being ready on time. Alec had gone without her. Although he didn't know the groom well and had met the bride only once or twice, he felt a responsibility. The groom was on the baseball team Alec had recently begun playing with, a bunch of guys who had known each other since high school. Alec had heard about the team through Mel, who lived in the same apartment complex as he and Rose. The groom had been harassed about getting married all through the ball season; nonetheless, Alec knew that on the big day moral support was not only in order, but expected.

After the ceremony, Alec had tried to figure out what to do about Rose. When he left the apartment Rose had been trying to feed the baby who was screaming and slapping at the spoon.

1

Rose wasn't speaking to him, so they hadn't made arrangements for the reception.

He had wanted her to come. People would suspect marriage problems if she didn't show up. After the ceremony, he tried to guess what she would be expecting, what arrangement she would have chosen if they had made one. He decided she would likely want to come in her own car. She had this silly idea that it was important always to have your own car. So you could get away, she said. It was absurd. He was her husband, for God's sake. What husband and wife go to parties in separate cars?

But things had gotten off to a bad start so he decided it was best to appease her. He had gone ahead to the hotel and phoned home, just to make sure. The babysitter answered. Yes, she said, Rose had left. In her own car.

She showed up at the reception just in time. People were being seated at the round tables for dinner. Someone had already asked him if he were alone, planning to seat him at a table of singles probably. He had said no, he was with his wife, and anxiously watched the door, keeping an eye on the tables as they filled up. He was hoping to sit with some of his new friends from the ball team, but their tables were already full. That bugged Alec. He hadn't wanted to risk sitting down without Rose in case she didn't show. Her absence would really be noticed then. He wondered if he'd be able to pull up another two chairs when she got there, but decided that wasn't possible. Maybe later, when things got less formal.

Until he saw the red dress, he had really wanted her there. He was even prepared to put up with her mood, be patient and give her time to relax after getting away from the baby. But when she finally breezed in in the red dress, he became instantly irritated. He hated the way she casually scanned the tables, picked one and sat down without consulting him. It was a funny table, probably the misfits, the couples who didn't have friends here. It was the only table with several empty chairs and no one seemed to know one another. There were three couples seated, still two empty chairs after Rose and Alec sat down.

"Where were you?" he asked. "I was afraid you weren't coming." He didn't tell her that he'd phoned.

She didn't answer.

"Did you want me to pick you up?" he asked. "I decided you'd probably want to bring your car."

She still didn't answer. Alec didn't ask her anything else because their table was too quiet and he was afraid the others would notice she wasn't speaking to him. It was embarrassing. He looked around the room and watched people at the other tables, talking and laughing, obviously having a good time. Why wasn't Rose like that? Why didn't she know how to have a good time?

She ate her salad, but she didn't touch her main course. Alec looked around the table to see if anyone was watching her. The plate had probably cost the bride's family twenty dollars. It was damned inconsiderate of her not to eat it. He knew Rose was always counting calories, but surely you could make an exception at a formal dinner. The woman in the fedora ate everything, even the baked potato. And she certainly wasn't overweight. Alec looked at Rose in the red dress and thought she was too thin anyway. She had big breasts and now, since she'd lost weight, her hips were too small for the rest of her. He noticed that she'd washed her hair and blow-dried it so that it was a frizzy bush around her head and down her back. Why did she do that? She looked like a gypsy. If there was a camp fire in the middle of the room, she could dance around it.

The woman on the other side of him was speaking to him. "Excuse me," she was saying. "Please pass the butter."

"Sorry," Alec said, handing it to her. "Guess I was day-dreaming."

The woman beside him was more attractive than the woman in the fedora. She had a softer, more feminine look, a pink dress and blond curls.

"I suppose we should introduce ourselves," Alec said. "I'm Alec Crosbey. Friend of the groom."

"I'm Sally Winter," the woman said. "This is my husband, Ted. I'm the bride's third cousin, once removed."

Ted reached across his wife to shake Alec's hand. He pumped vigorously, smiled widely. The guy's an insurance salesman, Alec thought. He introduced Rose to Sally and Ted and she extended her hand. Alec noticed that Sally hesitated before she took it. Probably not used to shaking hands, Alec thought. Why did Rose have to do that? It was like she was always trying to make a point.

Other people at the table began introducing themselves to the people next to them, and light conversations started up. The wine was passed again and Rose poured herself a full glass.

By the time dessert was served, several empty wine bottles had been taken away and several more brought by the waiters. Alec had had a good discussion with Sally about who was going to win the World Series. He loved running into a woman who knew something about baseball. Sally and Ted had recently driven all the way to Minneapolis to watch a major league game. They did that at least once a year. Ted looked at Rose and tried to picture her in the stands at a ball game. He couldn't see it. He looked at Sally and easily pictured her in shorts and a pink ball cap.

"We have some really great photographs," Sally said. "Ted has a telephoto lens. They really tell a story, you know, when you line them all up. Pictures of people in the stands. Action shots of the players. The telephoto lens is really terrific. Of course, I wouldn't know what to do with it. I'm not mechanically minded at all."

Almost as if he knew what they were discussing, a photographer appeared at their table and started snapping candid shots.

"Don't look at me," he said. "Just keep on talking."

Alec noticed that Rose picked up her wine glass and looked right at the camera. She tipped her head back and drained the glass. The flash went off several times.

"Great," the photographer said. "Terrific shot. Everybody's having a good time."

"Hey, buddy," Ted said. "You do this for a living?"

"No," the photographer said. "I'm the groom's brother-in-law. It's just kind of a hobby."

"I've got the same hobby," Ted said. "It's super isn't it? What kind of lens you using there? I've got this really great Pentax telephoto. Got my own dark room too. Built it myself."

"That's terrific," the photographer said. He seemed to be lingering on Rose, the shutter clicking repeatedly.

Great, thought Alec. Rose's black mood in the middle of the wedding photographs.

"Hey, over here," he said quickly, putting his arm around Sally and smiling broadly. The photographer would probably think he was an asshole, but it didn't matter. He'd never see him again after tonight.

4

"Hope you don't mind," he said to Ted, after the photographer took their picture and turned toward another table.

"Hell no," said Ted. "What are wedding parties for?"

"Excuse me." It was the woman in the fedora. She was looking at Alec. "I think I've seen you before," she said. "Do you by any chance work for the Omega Group?"

"Yes, I do," said Alec, surprised. "Do you?"

"Yes," she said. "In financial management. Third floor."

Now he knew who she was. It was the hat. He hadn't recognized her with the hat on. She must have her hair piled up under it, he thought. The woman he was thinking of had luscious long hair, almost down to her knees.

"Tina," the woman said. "Tina Harvey."

"Of course," said Alec. "This is my wife, Rose."

"Charmed," said Rose. Alec was glad she stayed seated and didn't get up and walk around the table to shake Tina's hand.

"This is Buck," said Tina, introducing the blond.

Buck? thought Alec. Who is he kidding?

"Pleased to meet you, Buck," Alec said. He was damned glad he was too far away to shake hands with him.

There was one other couple at the table, seated between Ted and Sally and Tina and Buck. Alec figured he might as well take the initiative and introduce himself. They were an older couple, friends of someone's parents probably. Their names were Ursula and Jerzy, and they had accents, eastern European Alec guessed. They were quiet people, didn't seem to want to talk. Still, Alec supposed he should say something conversational.

"Hot weather we've been having," he said.

"Yes," Jerzy said. "Very hot."

"Very hot," said his wife, nodding. "A lovely day for a wedding."

"Do you golf?" Alec asked Jerzy.

"No," Jerzy said.

"He has a weak heart," said Ursula.

"Not too weak," said Jerzy. "I just have to be a little careful. That's all."

Alec choked back laughter and wished he was sitting with someone who could share the joke. Rose, Alec saw, was stirring her chocolate mousse and hadn't heard. Well, it didn't matter. She had no sense of humour anyway.

Alec saw a man stand and move to the microphone at the head table. The photographer moved forward too, and knelt at the side of the room, preparing to catch on film the various toasters and storytellers and telegram readers. The man, the bride's uncle, started to speak, but before he even finished a sentence the clinking of glasses began and the bride and groom were forced to stand up and kiss. This continued for the entirety of the program and Alec was reminded of his and Rose's wedding four years ago. She had refused to kiss Alec, and each time the clinking started she had gotten up and kissed one of the clinkers. Funny, Alec thought, how you think you know someone. Then you find out you really didn't know them at all. He was sure that was it. She hadn't changed, she'd been like that all along. He wished he would have thought about it more before they got married. It turned out they really weren't suited to one another. He didn't even find her attractive. He stole a glance at her in the red dress. It was gauche.

He was relieved when the tables were cleared and the band set up for the dance. The lights would be turned down and everyone would relax. It wouldn't matter so much that Rose was inappropriately dressed and sulking. Maybe he would even leave her sitting with these people while he joined his friends.

The room was getting warm. Alec saw one of the waiters come in and tie back the heavy velvet drapes. It was an old hotel and the bay windows had not been sealed up. The waiter swung several of them open and Alec felt the cool breeze. It smelled like rain. The branches of a big old elm tree swayed gently outside the window.

The band played middle-of-the-road dance tunes and had a sunset painted on the bass drum. The bride and groom started it off, then the bride danced with her father and the groom with his mother. Slowly, other couples began leaving their tables to dance. Alec kept his eye on his friends, waiting for an opportunity to join them. But what should he do about Rose? He could hardly introduce her to his friends with her acting the way she was. Suddenly, he hated her. He wanted to rip the red dress off her, expose and humiliate her in front of this crowd. He glared at her openly now that the lights were down, despised her without caring who saw. A flash went off in his face, and the photographer was there again, taking more pictures of Rose. Good, thought Alec. Now that it was over, he didn't care what the camera caught. Bliss or animosity, what difference did it make? Alec saw a jagged streak of lightning through one of the open windows. He watched the tree and thought the breeze was turning into a wind.

Alec felt Rose's hand on his arm.

"Do you want to dance?" she asked.

Alec stared at her. What is she up to now, he wondered. After embarrassing him all through dinner, she decides she wants to dance. Well, it was too late. He didn't want to dance with her anyway, not in that whore's dress.

"No," he said.

"Fine," said Rose. She got up from the table and went to the bar. Alec watched her chatting with the bartender. She was flirting, he thought. She was probably asking him to dance. God damn her. When she returned to the table he took the drink out of her hand and set it on the table.

"All right," he said, standing. "I'll dance. But just one."

As they joined the small crowd of dancers, Alec had another attack of seething anger about Rose's dress. It was cut too low in the front, her breasts were bursting out over the top of the red material. Everyone in the room was probably staring at them, the men lusting, the women incensed. There was a spotlight above the hardwood dance floor, and Alec could see flashes of light, like fireflies, dancing around on Rose's body as she moved.

She was good. In school she had studied modern dance and jazz, and sometimes, when she got on a dance floor, she moved as though she were on stage. He used to think it was fun being married to such a good dancer, but now it was just one more embarrassment. The bride was supposed to be the centre attraction at a wedding. Not some tart in a red dress. Alec looked around the floor to see if the bride was dancing. Luckily, she wasn't.

It unnerved Alec that Rose stared at him while they danced, her eyes burning into his, her face set with strange determination, although determination to do what he hadn't a clue. The photographer was sneaking around the dance floor taking pictures, and Alec kept turning away from him. It became a game that kept his mind off Rose, watching the photographer and staying out of his viewfinder. But when the music ended the two of them caught him completely off guard. Rose put her arms around his neck and kissed him full on the mouth. A flash went off in his eyes and Alec heard a whoop from the table where his buddies were sitting. Furious, he grabbed Rose by the arm and hurried her off the dance floor and back to their dinner table.

He didn't know what to do. Play along with her for the rest of the evening? Or leave her on her own and let his buddies know he wasn't going to take any shit? He needed a few minutes to think about this, so he pulled out Rose's chair and sat down beside her.

"Hey," Ted said. "You two are really great dancers."

"Very good dancers," said Ursula, nodding agreement.

"Buck here is a good dancer," said Tina. "He teaches at the Arthur Murray School. I hate dancing with him because he makes me look so bad." Buck pretended to box her ears and she giggled.

"Ted won't dance," said Sally.

"Damn right I won't," said Ted. "Never have, never will."

"I'm going to the washroom," said Alec, standing, but before he could leave the photographer was there again.

"Wait. Wait a minute. Everybody squish together here for a quick shot. I need one of the whole table."

Alec sat down beside Rose and everyone shuffled their chairs around to one side of the table.

"Okay, smile. That's right. Good one. Terrific."

A giant clap of thunder shook the room as they moved their chairs back in place. A hotel attendant appeared and began to close the windows, but the bride hurried over and spoke to him, apparently asking to have them left open. He nodded and left the room again. Alec went to the washroom. In front of the urinal, he decided to leave Rose on her own. When he returned, he went to the table of ball players and sat down in an empty chair next to Mel.

"Alec, my man," said Mel holding out his open palm. "Give me five." Alec did, then he looked around the table. The men were all sitting on one side and the women had their chairs bunched together in a little group. They were talking and laughing about something. Probably Rose, Alec thought. He checked out their dresses. Not one of them was in red, and their necklines were all appropriately modest.

"Hey Mel," Alec said. "How long were you married?"

"Forty-seven days," said Mel. "Why? You got trouble?"

"I guess," said Alec. "I figure it's over."

"That's too bad. You got a kid, too, don't you?"

8

"Yeah."

Alec thought about his son. Before the baby was born he'd had fantasies about having a son. But it was a big let down when Rose brought the baby home from the hospital. The fantasies had disappeared and had never come back. Not even now that the baby was toddling around and learning to say a few words.

"I don't know, man," Mel said. "If I'd had a kid I maybe would have hung in there. Anyway, are you sure you know what you're doing? I saw that kiss she planted on you a while ago."

"She was just playing with me," Alec said.

There was another clap of thunder and Alec looked up to see Rose dancing with Buck. Buck had taken off his jacket and rolled up his shirt sleeves. He and Rose were dancing like they were the only ones on the floor. People were getting out of the way to give them more room.

"You're right," said Mel. "You got trouble. I wouldn't recommend taking that guy on, either. He's built like Arnold Schwarzenegger, for Christ's sake."

When the song was over, Buck spoke to the band. They stepped up the pace with the next tune, and Buck and Rose went wild. The skirt of Rose's dress swirled out from her thighs as she spun around and around, pulling away from Buck, then letting him draw her back so closely that their bodies touched.

At first Alec looked away. But when he heard people around him clapping, he looked back toward the dance floor. There was no one there but Buck and Rose. The other dancers, even the bride and groom, were sidelined. Then Buck dropped back and Rose was alone under the spotlight, twirling in the red dress, doing pirouettes and kicking high above her head. The photographer was on his knees again, snapping furiously.

"Hey Alec," someone yelled from across the table. "Your wife is dynamite."

There was suddenly a brilliant flash of lightning and a simultaneous crack of thunder followed by an eerie cracking sound outside. The band stopped, and people sitting near the windows jumped up as the huge tree wavered, then crashed to the ground away from the building.

A crowd of people, Alec among them, rushed to the windows to see where the tree had landed. It was lying across several cars in the lighted parking lot below. Miraculously, it had missed

9

the power lines. The rain was coming straight down in huge drops.

"Christ," a man next to Alec said. "I think it's flattened a Porsche."

Alec felt someone shoving behind him. It was the photographer, and he pushed his way to the window and leaned out. Other people were shoving to get a look at the tree and check to see if their own cars were under it. Alec was glad he'd parked on the street.

People began appearing in the parking lot, plastic bags, jackets, and umbrellas over their heads. They gathered around the tree like curious cats, peering under it. One man looked up at the hotel windows and shouted, "Anyone up there drive a yellow Porsche? She's a mess."

The camera shutter clicked several times in Alec's ear. Alec had the urge to give the photographer a shove and send him and his camera to the pavement. He watched as a man in tails ran through the rain to the Porsche, shouting something. The little throng of people moved out of the way and the man stepped up to what appeared to be the remains of his car.

Then Alec saw the red dress. Rose was walking through the parking lot in the rain, bare arms, nothing on her head, hair drenched and hanging down her back. Alec could see her Volkswagen Rabbit at the far end of the lot, untouched by the tree. She stopped when she saw the man in front of his car, then walked toward him. They exchanged a few words. Rose put her arms around him and lay her head against him. Alec's face burned, but he couldn't turn away.

Rose took her arms away from the man and began to walk toward her car.

"Hey. Up here."

It was the photographer again, calling down to Rose. How did she know he was yelling at her? She did though, because she stopped and turned toward the windows. She tossed back her hair, placed her hands provocatively on her hips, and posed for the camera. There were cat calls and whistles from the other open windows in the hotel.

"Got it," the photographer yelled and waved.

Alec pushed back through the crowd to get away from the window. Had she seen him? Did she do that especially for him? Bitch.

WEAK HEARTS

There was no one sitting at the table where the ball players had been. Alec couldn't see his friends anywhere and figured they must be on the way down to check their cars. The couples he and Rose had had dinner with were still at their table, sitting as though nothing had happened. Buck had his jacket back on and he and Tina were engaged in some kind of foreplay, pecking at each other's lips. Ted and Sally appeared to be having an argument. Jerzy and Ursula sat with their hands in their laps, staring straight ahead as though they had nothing to say to anyone. Alec caught Ursula's eye as he pulled out a chair and sat down.

"Very good dancer," she said. "Your wife is a very good dancer. Is she a professional?"

Alec shook his head. The camera appeared in front of his face again, and he heard the now familiar voice from behind the flash of light.

"Great shots. Fabulous. There. That about wraps it up."

THE WINTER ROAD

I'd seen her once or twice, but I'd never paid much attention to her before tonight. Duff figures she's one of those people who have their signals jammed up. She's really something to watch, though, one foot after the other in all this snow like there's nothing to it. If it wasn't so silly I'd say she was like a camel crossing a desert. Maybe that's not so silly. It *is* like a desert, a cold white one. I don't know how I got here. It just sort of happened.

I often go over to Stella's in the evening to help her get the kids to bed. That's where I was tonight and when I got home, there was my suitcase, sitting on the front step half covered with snow. I tried the porch door but it was locked. I knew Duff was inside because I could hear the TV, but when I knocked he didn't answer. I took off my mitts and opened the suitcase to see what was inside. Beer bottle caps. Nothing else. Just the bottle caps I'd been saving in a box in the closet. I sat down on the step and tried to figure out what it meant.

The curtains were pulled but I could picture Duff slouched in his chair, his feet in grey work socks up on the coffee table. He would be staring at the TV, smoking one cigarette after another, blowing smoke rings out in front of him, thinking about who knows what. Earlier tonight, I watched him from the kitchen doorway and I could have sworn he was going to jump up and put his foot right through the TV screen. It was like something was cooking inside him, just about ready to boil over, just a fraction of an inch from blowing the top off the pan. "Is it me?" I asked him. "Are you tired of me?" He didn't answer. I wondered at the time about his not answering, and decided it meant I'd asked a stupid question. Later, sitting on the step, I knew it

13

wasn't a stupid question. That was what the suitcase was all about. He was kicking me out.

It was cold, at least twenty below, and the snow was coming down and I had maybe seventy-five cents in my pocket. I just sat there on the step, the cold coming through my jeans, the snow piling up on me like I was part of the outside, something that gets covered up and stays that way until spring. Me and the suitcase, just two lumps of snow on Duff's front step.

I couldn't go to Stella's house. Once I tried to stay with her when Duff's party got too loud and I was tired. I sneaked out, thinking there were so many people packed into the house he would never miss me. Stella told me to go back home, she wasn't going to have me staying there and making her explain to her kids why I was on the couch and not home in my own house where I should be. "Get your life in order," Stella told me. "I'm not bailing anybody out who won't stick up for herself like she's got a right to. That's your house too. Go home and kick them all out." Stella would do that. Not me. I couldn't.

And there I was, kicked out in the cold. I sort of shuffled my feet on the step and stamped a bit, hoping Duff would hear me and maybe have a change of heart. But he wasn't going to and I knew it. He was done with me.

I tried to see the lake through the trees. In the summer I would sit on the step and think about the lake going on forever, like they say the ocean does. It made me feel I was at the beginning of something, something that had no end. And it felt good to think about that, to think maybe there is something in life that's got no end. Just maybe.

The ocean is where I was headed when I met Duff. I had my suitcase, the same one, and I was heading west. I could have gone straight from Montana to Oregon or California, but I figured if I came to Canada they wouldn't be able to find me. Not that they'd bother looking, but just in case. It made me kind of sad to think about that. I wasn't going back to Montana, not ever, but it would've been nice if somebody cared.

I couldn't see the lake. It was too dark and the snow was coming down too hard. All I could see was a black line of trees across the road and Duff's taxi parked off to the side like always, attached to the yellow extension cord that ran under the snow from a little hole in the porch door.

I must have looked at that taxi for a good half-hour. Maybe

14

it was Duff's turning out the lights just then that made me decide to take it. I watched to see if he was going to peek through the curtains and check on me, but he didn't. Has he really quit thinking about me already, I wondered, or is he just making sure I know he means it? One way or the other, it didn't matter. I was cold and the taxi was there with the keys under the front seat where Duff always tossed them. I picked up the suitcase and walked out to the road. I stopped more than once and looked at the house, hoping to see Duff at the window, grinning, waving for me to come back and get into bed and he would get in too and keep me warm. But the curtains were closed up tight and they stayed that way. I threw the suitcase in the taxi and even after I started it up I sat there, waiting, the windshield wipers making two little half-circle windows. Finally I drove away, thinking about the suitcase behind me on the back seat. At least it's mine, I thought. At least I'm taking something with me that's mine. Even if it is just an old suitcase full of bottle caps.

That town has only one road and whichever way you go, north or south, the next town is a long way off. Less than a quarter tank is how much gas Duff's taxi had in it, and that wasn't going to get me very far. I was nervous too, not having driven more than once or twice since I came here. The town is small and you can walk anywhere you want to go. Unless you live on the reserve or in one of the cabins along the lake north of town. That's how Duff mostly makes his living – driving those people back and forth. Sometimes he drives people all the way to one of the cities in the south. Then you don't see him for a few days, maybe even a week. He stays and has a good time.

It didn't change my life any, when Duff went away on his trips. I just kept on doing the same things. Reading magazines. Watching TV. Playing with Stella's kids. "Maybe I should have a kid," I said to Stella once. "Don't you dare," she told me. "You get your life in order first. Don't you dare have a kid, thinking that will make everything better." So I didn't. I didn't bring it up and neither did Duff.

Whenever Duff went away I got out the bottle caps. I have this idea you should be able to make something out of them. They're too nice to throw in the garbage or leave lying around outside to rust. "What are you saving those for?" Duff would ask me. I'd always look away, not wanting him to think I was stupid. He'd laugh then, but I liked it because it was the kind of laugh that said I was all right.

Once when Duff was away I got out all the bottle caps I'd saved and laid them, one at a time, on the counter top in the kitchen. I thought I might glue them down someday and put plaster around them the way you do with tiles. I spent the whole afternoon moving them around, making different patterns, thinking how unique it would be for a counter top, how maybe I could take a picture and send it to one of those decorating magazines. But I never did get it done. Just as well now, I thought. A handmade counter top would only have made it harder to leave.

I drove past the turnoff to Stella's house. I couldn't see lights through the trees, though, so I kept on going. North. Clear to the other end of town. When I passed the last house I stopped the car, turned out the lights, and stared into the blackness. Only a fool would head out in that snow, I thought, even if she did have a full tank of gas. And south was the direction I should be headed in. Back the way I came. Back to the trans-Canada highway where I could head for the ocean again. Vancouver. I could get some kind of job where you don't need work papers. Babysitting, maybe. Stella always says I'm good with kids. I could head south, find that same grid road, just pick up where I left off when Duff came along in his taxi.

I was walking, carrying my old suitcase. The sun was going down and I was wondering where I was going to sleep, wondering if the ditch was dry enough and if there were rattlesnakes in Saskatchewan. Duff pulled up beside me. He was on his way back from driving someone all the way to Malta, Montana for a good time.

"You want a lift?" he said to me, leaning across the seat and looking at me through the open passenger window.

"Where you going?" I asked.

"Wherever you're going, little darlin'," he said.

"I'm going west," I said. "To Vancouver."

He didn't say anything right away and I looked in the window at him, not knowing whether he wanted me to get in or not. He was grinning and he had on a brand new cowboy hat, a tall one with a big blue feather plastered across the front. I remember the wind blowing my hair into my eyes and my mouth and I stood there pulling it away with one hand and holding the suitcase with the other. When he took so long to say something I got scared that he was thinking I was too young, that he might call the police, or take me back to the border. Then he laughed. He reminded me of somebody's brother. No one in particular. Just someone who might tease you or call you funny nicknames.

"Get in," he said. "I'll drive you to Vancouver."

"I don't have any money to pay you," I said after I was settled in the car.

"That's okay," he said. "I'll pay you."

He did too. The first motel we came to he pulled in and handed me a fifty dollar bill.

"What's this for?" I said, looking at the bill, then at Duff in his new cowboy hat.

"Don't you know?" he said. "God damn. I figured any girl out on the road by herself would know what this is for."

I thought about being in Canada on my way to Vancouver. I needed the money.

"I guess I know," I said, stuffing the bill in my jeans pocket. "But just remember, I'm no whore."

That night in the motel I lay awake long after Duff fell asleep. I lay on my back close to the edge of the bed, my arms at my sides. I could feel the sheets touching me all over, cold and starchy. I was afraid to move. I had thoughts in my head that I didn't want. About babies left behind, about Charity taking my place as the oldest and what she was in for. But I knew she would be stronger than me.

Duff slept for a couple of hours, then woke up and in the light coming through the window he could see I was still awake.

"Jesus," he said. "You're lying there like a piece of plywood. What the hell's the matter?"

"I can't sleep," I said. "I've never slept without my nightgown. I think I should put it on."

He sat up and stared at me.

"Well, Jesus," he said. "Get up and put the damned thing on."

I did. I could tell he was watching me and I was embarrassed but I pulled my nightgown on and got into bed again. I lay on my back close to the edge of the bed and he moved over beside me. He put one arm over me and moved his head into my neck. He was warm. I closed my eyes and went to sleep.

The next morning Duff said we should get married. We were eating breakfast at this little cafe called Nik and Karol's. Duff

17

had finished off four fried eggs and was waiting for another two. I was trying my best to eat at least one egg, when out of the blue Duff said we should get married. I told him I didn't have any legal papers or anything and he said that didn't matter, he knew a preacher who'd marry us anyway. I asked Duff where he lived and he told me about the lake. I'd never thought about lakes. When he told me you could see the lake from his front door and you couldn't see the other side it was so big, I decided to go with him.

We drove all day, north out of the prairie, through rolling hills and on into the bush country. When we got there, I could see Duff wasn't lying about the lake. I walked across the road to the shore and I looked out over miles and miles of water. You couldn't see the other side.

Duff wasn't lying about the preacher either. He lived in an old church and had driven all the way to California to get ordained. He didn't care about papers or blood tests or anything else and we got married that same night. Duff called up some of his friends and threw a party at the house. I tried to stay in the bathroom but people kept pounding on the door and I'd have to come out. Stella was there. She was still married to Gator then and was trying to keep tabs on him by not letting him go out alone.

"I don't know where you come from," she said to me that night, "but you are some crazy girl to come up here and get married to Duff."

"He seems all right," I said.

"You come and see me if you need company," she said. "I got three kids who like it when someone comes over. And don't let Duff get away with being an asshole."

"At least I'm married," I said. "I sure never thought that was going to happen."

I drove back into town and parked in front of the hotel. I had a quarter-tank of gas and no money. And I had to leave town before morning if I was going in Duff's taxi. Maybe I should just take it home, I thought, walk back to the hotel and beg for a room. Or maybe I could go and wake up Stella. If I told her about the suitcase on the step maybe she'd let me stay there for the night and lend me bus fare in the morning.

Someone opened the passenger door.

18

"I need a lift," a woman's voice said from inside a furry parka hood. "Can you take me a few miles down the road?"

"No," I said, not bothering to explain that I wasn't the taxi driver. "Too much snow." I waited for her to shut the door and go away. But she didn't. She climbed in and pulled a fifty dollar bill out of her pocket.

"Fifty bucks for a short trip," she said. "That's a pretty good fare."

Fifty bucks. That would buy me a tank of gas or a bus ticket to somewhere. It was pitch dark and cold and snowing like crazy. I needed the money.

"You sure it's only a few miles?" I asked.

"Positive," she said, tossing back her parka hood.

I recognized her. She was the woman who walked all over. Duff had pointed her out and said he figured she was crazy. He said he'd seen her twenty miles from nowhere in the middle of the night. That's what kind of night Duff picks to get tired of me, I thought. Even the walking woman wants a ride.

I had to see Stella. I knew I was going to take that fifty dollars and fill Duff's taxi up with gas and head south before morning.

"Do you mind waiting in the car for a few minutes?" I asked the woman. "I've got to stop and see someone."

"No problem," she said. "As long as you leave it running so I can listen to the radio."

"Jesus," Stella said. "It's two o'clock in the morning. I thought I said you can't stay here."

"I don't want to stay," I said. "I just want to talk for a few minutes."

Stella looked past me, out into the snow.

"Isn't that Duff's taxi out front?" she asked.

"Yeah," I said. "Can I come in for a few minutes?"

"Is Duff out there?" she asked, closing the door after me. "He's not going to come busting in here and wake up the kids, is he?"

Stella has four kids now, the last one born two months after Gator left, a baby girl. I stayed with the other three while she was in the hospital. She stayed in overnight then went right home because she was afraid Gator might come back while she was gone. I tried to get her to name the baby Charity. "What the hell kind of name is that?" she said and called her Marlene.

19

"Duff's going to drive around a bit, then pick me up," I said. "He won't come in."

"Well how long is he going to drive around for?" Stella asked. "I mean, should I make coffee or what?"

"No," I said. "Better not make coffee. He won't be that long."

I stood there in the kitchen and looked at the snow melting on my boots and tried to think of what to say. Stella stood there in her blue terry cloth housecoat, hands on her hips, fierce and protective. She would kill Gator if he tried to hurt those kids. I know it.

I wanted to tell her what was going on, but I didn't know how to say it. How could I tell Stella I was heading for the ocean with a suitcase full of bottle caps? Was that getting your life in order? I didn't figure Stella would think so.

I was looking at the crayon drawings taped to the fridge when something came to me. "I wanted to check on when the kids' birthdays are," I said. I thought about the four of them in their beds and I knew this was different from the last time I set out for the ocean. I didn't want Stella and her kids to think I was dead.

"Jesus," Stella said, slapping her hand down on the kitchen counter. "You come over here in the middle of the night to check on when the kids' birthdays are. That beats everything. You were crazy when you came here, but living with Duff has made you even crazier."

"I was just thinking about how I should get them all a birthday present," I said. "I should have done that last year. I should have been doing it all along, don't you think?"

Stella stared at me. "What are you up to?" she finally said. "Have you been out drinking with Duff?"

I started to laugh. I laughed until Stella told me to be quiet, I was going to wake up the kids. Then she tore a slip of paper off the notepad by the telephone, wrote the kids' birthdates on it and handed it to me.

"Thanks," I said, stuffing it in my coat pocket. I stood there trying to think of one more thing to say, something really important for Stella to remember me by. Nothing came.

"Shit," Stella finally said. She put her arms around me and gave me a hug. "Go home," she whispered.

The reception on the radio was terrible.

"You should have a tape deck," the woman said. "The reception's always bad up here."

"Maybe I'll get one," I said. I didn't want to tell her it wasn't my taxi.

Stella's house was just off the main road and when we got to the intersection I asked the woman which way she wanted to go, north or south.

"Neither," she said. "East is where I want to go."

East, I thought, trying to figure out in my head if there was any road east except the winter road across the lake.

"East," she said. "The winter road."

I saw the money slipping away. I should have known, I thought. She's crazy, just like Duff said. That's why she walks all over the place. She's walking the demons out, or whatever it is that makes people get that way. There's nothing along that winter road, I thought. Nothing but forty-five miles of snowplow trail across the ice. I knew there was a town on the other side, but I wasn't driving forty-five miles across a frozen lake in a snow storm no matter how much she wanted to pay me.

"There's nothing a few miles out on that winter road," I said. "Just ice and snow. And I sure don't have enough gas to get us all the way across the lake."

"There's a cabin," she said. "On an island. The road goes right by it. If it wasn't snowing you could see the lights from here."

I thought about that. It was true, you could sometimes see lights from cabins out on the lake. Some people had gas generators to supply them with power.

"Is that where you live?" I asked.

"No," she said. "But I've got an important appointment. It can't wait until tomorrow."

I looked at her and she didn't look crazy. She looked like a woman with something that had to be done. And she had fifty dollars and three miles wasn't very far.

"We'll just head out that way and see what the road looks like," I said. "If it's bad, we're not going."

She nodded.

The snowplow had cut a wide trough on the lake. The snow was drifted in on the sides, but the road was still passable. Every once in a while we'd come to a spot where the snow was deeper and you could hear it hitting the bottom of the car. The windshield wipers were still making their little half-circle windows and the headlights lit an eerie path down the trough.

"As long as we don't meet another car we should be all right," I said.

"Nobody else will be out on a night like this," the woman said. It was warm in the car and she unzipped her parka.

"We must be just about there," I said.

She yawned and leaned her head back against the seat. I watched the mileage. The snow was coming out of the blackness, icy pellets coming straight at us then veering off to either side. It was warm in the car but I could feel the cold just the same and I thought about another night in the cold. Charity and I and the three little ones in the car, parked in a farmyard somewhere, waiting for him to come out. They were crying, the three of them, and Charity and I were trying to keep them warm. The rear window was broken and the snow was coming in on the back seat so we all got in the front and huddled together. "That son-of-a-bitch," Charity kept saying and I was worried the boys could hear her and they might tell. I couldn't feel my hands anymore. "I'm going in there," Charity said and I tried to stop her but she went anyway. He came out on the step and hit her and then pushed her across the yard all the way to the car, hitting her. She was falling and getting up again and then he threw her right across the car hood and went back inside. Charity got in the car and we all huddled together again and I was crying and she had blood on her face and hands. "Shut up," she said to me. "You're supposed to be the oldest. Quit bawling like a baby. It's just a little bit of blood." But I couldn't stop crying and through the windshield all I could see was black going on forever and that was where I wanted to be.

I stopped the car. The woman was asleep beside me.

"All right," I said. "You better wake up. We've gone more than three miles and I haven't seen any sign of a cabin. Are you sure we can see it if the lights are off?"

"Can't miss it," she said, peering out into the snow. "We mustn't have come to it yet. Just try a bit farther."

I had no choice. I couldn't turn around. She knew what I was thinking.

"It's okay," she said. "The snowplow always makes an extra swipe in toward the island. You'll be able to turn around there."

Another mile, I decided. If that didn't get us to the cabin, I was putting Duff's taxi in reverse and backing all the way to town. Just one more mile. The walking woman leaned her head back and went to sleep again and the snow kept piling up on the road. Pretty soon you could hear the bottom of the car dragging all the time and I knew I wasn't going to be able to back up five yards without getting stuck. So I kept going. I kept driving until the car slowed down and then stopped altogether. I spun the tires a few times, then turned off the ignition. The woman woke up.

"It doesn't matter," I said to her. "We're just about out of gas anyway."

"Time to walk then," she said, zipping up her parka. "I hope you had the sense to wear warm clothes. It's a bitch out there tonight."

I zipped up my own coat and searched my pockets for a toque. I felt the slip of paper with Stella's kids' birthdates written on it.

"Here," the woman said when she was set to go. She handed me the fifty dollars. I wrapped the car keys in it and tossed it under the seat.

You'd think it would be cold out here, but it's not. Walking in the dark with all this snow coming down makes you feel like you're inside a glass ball, the kind with a little scene inside and you shake it up and all this white stuff floats around. Someone has to keep shaking it up, though. That's the difference. Here it just keeps coming down all by itself.

I can't see her anymore. She walks so fast I can't keep up to her. The suitcase is slowing me down too. She laughed at me for bringing it along but I didn't want to leave it in the car. Duff would just throw it out.

For a while I was following her footsteps, but now she's so far ahead of me the snow is filling them in. It doesn't matter. It's pretty hard to get lost when you're walking in a trough. Maybe there is something up ahead. The town. The cabin we were looking for. If it wasn't snowing I could probably see the lights, just like the woman said.

I used to stand on the shore in front of Duff's house and look out across the lake, thinking that it had no end, thinking it went on and on forever. I never thought about the winter road before tonight. I don't suppose there's anything in the world that has no end. Not even the ocean.

THE WEDNESDAY
FLOWER MAN

This afternoon Dennis will be delivering, for the last time, the usual box of roses to the apartment on Ninety-first Street. I wonder if he'll be doing anything special to commemorate the occasion. Probably not. I wonder who they'll hire to take his place. Who Dennis will hire to take his own place, I should say. It burns me even to think about it.

When I got to work this morning I found out Dennis got Mrs. Boyle's job as manager of the shop. The delivery boy for Christ's sake. All this time I thought Lila was my only competition, Lila with her four hundred dollar suits and her phony fingernails. I didn't even think about Dennis. What does he know about helping people select the right arrangement for the right occasion? What does he know about weddings and funerals and how to let flowers do your talking for you? I'm the one who's good at that. I'm better than Lila was, too. Just as good as Mrs. Boyle. It makes me wonder who's making the damned decisions in this world. It makes me wonder if there's anybody at the wheel.

I suppose that incident with the swearing could have had something to do with it. Mrs. Boyle did have to speak to me because a customer complained. Some old biddy wanted to have lilies for her husband's funeral. He wasn't even dead yet. It just so happened I had heard about a funeral where they had lilies all over the place, tons of them, and a lot of people were allergic to them. So I told her I wouldn't recommend lilies. I told her you can't have a proper funeral with everyone sneezing their goddamned heads off. She was offended by the goddamned. Not appropriate when dealing with a grieving public, Mrs. Boyle said to me, so I watched myself from then on. It just goes to show, a mistake follows you around, even if it's a little one. The more I think about it, the more I think the swearing incident must be why Dennis got the job and not me.

It was Lila who made me want to swear, right from the day she started working at the shop. Pinching the dead leaves off plants with her clipper-like fingernails. Buying a new tailored suit every payday. Answering the phone so efficiently: "Good morning. Flowers on the Avenue. Lila speaking. May I help you?" It made me sick. She was all fake, and there's nothing that makes me sicker than a person who lacks sincerity. She didn't really want to help anybody. Take the Wednesday flower man, for instance. Lila decided he was a fruitcake and wouldn't answer the phone at all before lunch on the last Wednesday of the month.

I never used to swear, at least not much. The four and a half years I was married to Howard I'll bet I never swore more than once or twice. Of course I was young then, right out of high school. Howard and I fell in love in the high school parking lot. His grandmother left him her car when she died and he used to sit in it all by himself before the bell rang and after school. It was a big car, a four-door Chev sedan; it had room for a whole pile of kids, but no one ever sat with him. I guess everybody figured he was kind of dippy, which he was, but at the same time he had this cute lock of blond hair which kept falling over one eye. It wasn't left long intentionally. Howard wasn't that cool. Maybe the barber just kept forgetting to cut it. Maybe he'd get Howard in his chair and he'd get so bored he'd gaze out the window and forget what he was doing. Howard could do that to you. But even so, you could forgive him. He was a real nice guy, not the kind of guy to make you want to swear.

I climbed into his car with him one day and we fell in love. We decided we should get married right after graduation because we couldn't wait any longer. With that big back seat in his grandmother's Chev, there was a lot of temptation to resist.

Howard thought we should get an apartment and he would go to school for two years and get his business diploma. His grandmother had left him some money in her will. I wanted to go to California with it, see Disneyland and Universal Studios and hang out on the beach watching the surfers, but Howard said his grandmother had wanted him to go to school so that's what he did. He went to school and I stayed in the apartment and hung wallpaper and made spaghetti and meatballs for

supper. After Howard got his diploma he found a job right off
selling pills and stuff to doctors.

I didn't think he would do very well at a sales job, but he really
tied into it and surprised the hell out of everybody. He read
his text books so many times he practically had them memorized.
And he got magazine subscriptions and read out loud to me
about how some guy or other said you could increase your sales.
He even dreamed about selling. Once I tried to tell him we should
take a trip around the world on a freighter and he looked at
me as if I were crazy.

Howard was on the road a lot so I stocked up on frozen meat
pies for myself and started living for *The Edge of Night* on
daytime TV. There was a woman named April that I wanted
to be like. She had soft blond hair and a curvy figure and everybody loved her. I took to dressing as much like her as I could
and I spoke in a soft voice, which confused Howard at first but
he got used to it.

The funny thing was, the more April became unhappy on *The
Edge of Night*, the more unhappy I became in our apartment.
After a while April's sadness started to get to me. I figured out
I wasn't the least bit like her. "Quit moping around," I wanted
to yell at her. "You're too soft. Toughen up a little." I took to
writing letters to the TV station. I took to secretly writing scripts
in which April got tough. But she never did and finally one day
I just up and left. I took some money from our account and
left. Poor Howard. He arrived home and no me, just magazine
subscriptions and frozen meat pies. He needed me too. I know
he did. I was a damned good woman to come home to.

Well, one thing is certain. I didn't leave Howard eleven years
ago to end up a nobody in a flower shop for the rest of my life.
I left Howard so I could travel around the world having affairs,
maybe starring in a movie or two, meeting suspicious characters
in smoky bars and being asked to smuggle heroin or diamonds
across the border. I wouldn't have done anything too illegal,
but just to be asked would have been something.

Actually, none of that happened. I took enough of Howard's
money to go to Europe, but I chickened out at the airport and
spent the money on a used Camaro instead, a real beauty. I had
it painted hot pink. A year ago some young kid side-swiped it
on the street, totalled it. Sometimes I really miss that car.

After I didn't go to Europe, I worked seasonal on the city

parks maintenance crew. That lasted for six years. Then I saw the flower shop job ad saying *chance for advancement*, and I remembered something Howard used to say. "No sense having a job where you get stuck on the middle rung of the ladder. If you can't see your way clear to the top, look elsewhere." It had worked for Howard. When I left him he was well on his way. Twice in a row he'd been salesman of the year for his pharmaceutical company. Howard would have been proud of me, I figured, going after a job where I could move up. Not that I cared what Howard thought, but after you've lived with somebody for a few years some of their favourite sayings stick with you. I applied for the job and got it. The chance for advancement was Mrs. Boyle's age and I thought it was a sure thing.

Of course Lila thought that too. When Mrs. Boyle and the head office people decided we could use more staff, they put another ad in the paper saying *chance for advancement* and Lila made it clear her first day on the job what her intentions were.

That's another thing I hated about Lila, she tried so damned hard. She'd read books, she said, about how you should dress and act if you wanted to get ahead. That's what the suits were all about. She asked me once if I thought she should continue having her nails done, if they were maybe a little garish for her image, which was obviously conservative.

"How should I know?" I said. "You're the one who's read all the goddamned books."

"I'm trying to be friendly," Lila said to me then, getting this phony hurt look on her face. "I like to think I can be friends with my co-workers."

Stupid, I figure. You can't be friends with the competition. Still, I feel just a little bad hating Lila now that she's dead. Not liking someone and hating them are two different things. And I hated her. Of course, I didn't tell the police that. I figured they'd be around asking Dennis and me and Mrs. Boyle what we thought of Lila and whether or not we'd like to see her dead. I was planning to lie because I was afraid they'd think I did it. Lucky for me there's been a whole rash of murders in the last six months. When the police came around, they asked if Lila had said anything about being afraid, about being followed or getting strange phone calls or anything like that. They weren't very creative in their questioning. They hardly paid any attention to us at all. If I were a cop I'd have explored a few avenues they didn't touch. Like, did any of us stand to gain from Lila's death? Did one of us have any reason for wanting her out of the way, for leaving her dead in a dark alley? Those are just standard questions, for God's sake. Anyway, we told them Lila hadn't said anything about any strange events, and they weren't surprised. They weren't expecting to hear anything that would help them, and when they left they said they figured Lila was just another woman in the wrong place at the wrong time.

"You watch yourselves," the youngest cop (he still had puberty pimples) said to me and Mrs. Boyle. "This guy is sick. He doesn't care who his victims are. Your Lila was young and pretty, but from what I've seen anybody will do."

Mrs. Boyle thought that was funny. She laughed herself silly over it. I should have been glad to hear her laugh because ever since she got the letter saying when she'd have to retire she'd been really depressed. She figured the company should have let her go on working because her eyesight and all that was still good, but when she wrote a letter about it they told her it was company policy and they couldn't make any exceptions because then everybody would want to keep working and where would that get them? It put me in a kind of awkward position. I felt sorry for Mrs. Boyle and I knew she could keep working and do a good job. But I wanted a promotion. I wanted to be a manager and I was sick of waiting. It really burned me when I heard Lila telling her she should go to the Human Rights Commission, maybe take the company to court and set a precedent. Really stupid, I thought. You're not getting any younger, I wanted to say to her. You want Mrs. Boyle to work till she's ninety-five? Where will that get us? A big waste of your expensive suits, I wanted to say.

That young cop made Mrs. Boyle laugh like she wasn't sixty-five, but I was so mad I had to go into the back room for an hour. I sat on a stool and looked at the glass vases lined up on the shelves waiting for flowers and it was all I could do to keep from swiping at the whole lot of them. Me, the one who thought she could star in a movie, in the same category as Mrs. Boyle with her white hair and polyester pantsuits. There was a mirror in the back room and I had a good look at myself in it.

The truth is, the young cop was right. Lila was pretty and I wasn't. I had never been pretty, not even when Howard fell in love with me. Mrs. Boyle had probably never been pretty either. She would have been one of those girls who have some feature that makes them stick out as being weird or unnaturally ugly. Like a really big nose. Or an especially long neck. Or hair so thin you're sure they're going to go bald before they go grey. I couldn't pick out any particular feature on Mrs. Boyle now that she was old, but I was sure she'd had one when she was younger.

Sitting on a stool in the back room, I looked at the row of vases waiting for flowers and wondered how she ever got to be Mrs. Boyle instead of staying Miss Boyle for her whole life. I wondered where Mr. Boyle came from. Mail order, I decided. Mrs. Boyle's father got worried when she turned twenty-seven or so and was still unmarried, so he started looking through magazines for a mail-order husband from the Philippines. Those magazines have mostly girls, I know, but there must be a few men who'll marry anybody to get into Canada. And that's where Mr. Boyle came from and then he probably died from some Canadian disease he had no immunity to. Thinking about that was really depressing. To be one of those girls who have such a hard time finding anybody to marry, and then finding one who up and dies. And me put in the same category as one of those girls by some stupid pimply-faced excuse for a cop. It was almost too much to bear. I wanted to scream, "I had one once, and it was me who left. Me. Not him." But I started to cry instead and Mrs. Boyle had to send me home for the afternoon. She thought I was upset about Lila.

That's the good thing about people like Mrs. Boyle. They sometimes turn into mothering types. Her sort of looking out for me is what made me think she liked me especially, led me to believe I had the job for sure.

I didn't think of it at the time, but Dennis probably saw my going home that day as a golden opportunity. Who knows what happened after I left. He probably stepped in and hustled around to help Mrs. Boyle out and make a good impression, try to get her to like him as much as she likes me. I thought Dennis was just one of those good-looking, friendly kids who don't have a whole lot going on between their ears. Then he turns around and stabs me in the back. It just goes to show, you can't trust anybody.

It's almost lunch time and the flower man should be phoning soon. Business has been slow this morning and Dennis is hanging around in the back room with Mrs. Boyle. If he hasn't many deliveries he'll likely be hanging around out front all afternoon trying to look like a manager. Well, he's going to need a lot of practice. Dennis looks about as much like a manager as some high school kid just off the basketball court. I suppose I'll have to get used to him. If I decide to stay, that is. Maybe I'll apply for his delivery job. If I were the truck driver I'd get to take the roses to the apartment on Ninety-first Street. That would be something.

I've been thinking about that man for the whole two years he's been one of our customers. I've held off asking questions, though, because I figured you couldn't pry into a customer's personal affairs if you wanted to be manager of the shop. I do know the apartment is empty. Dennis found that out after no one answered the door three months in a row. He asked the caretaker, who said the apartment had been empty for several years, but that a man continued to pay rent on it. Dennis wanted to stop delivering the flowers after that, but Mrs. Boyle said he had to. The man made us promise.

It occurs to me I don't have anything to lose anymore. I'm sure as hell not going to hang around here until Dennis retires, then have the telephone repairman become the manager instead of me. Why shouldn't I pry, poke around a bit, ask the flower man a question or two? It wouldn't hurt, of course, to exercise a little discretion. I do have an apartment to keep up, groceries to buy, payments to make on my television set. I don't get any money from Howard, never have. Not that I deserve any after deserting him in his hour of need. And his hour of need is just what it was. That old saying is true. Behind every good man is a good woman. And Howard's good woman up and walked out on him when he was getting close to the top of the ladder, just when he needed her most. Maybe he didn't show that he was suffering on the surface; Howard wouldn't. But inside, he ached for me. He probably checked the obituaries every night in the paper, maybe still does. He probably called the police and reported a missing person. He may even have hired a private investigator. Not that that would have helped him. I didn't just walk out; I really went out of my way not be found, dyed my hair and changed my name and everything. I feel kind of bad about that now. I didn't have to go to that much trouble to keep Howard from tracking me down. I should have given him at least a sporting chance.

As it was, he couldn't stand living in that apartment without me. He couldn't even stand keeping the same job. I tried to call him a month or so after I'd left, just to see how he was doing. The number was "no longer in service". I called his boss and he told me Howard didn't work there anymore. I drove around in my Camaro looking for him, worried sick about what I'd done to him. Every once in a while I'd catch sight of him somewhere, but whenever I'd get close he'd disappear.

The telephone rings just before noon, right on time. I don't have to worry about Dennis rushing out to take the call. Dennis, like Lila, figures the man's a kook with enough money to throw forty bucks down the garbage chute every month. I don't think he's a kook. I think he's a man with a broken heart. He's been devastated by someone, a woman, and he's suffering, hurting where most people don't even have places. You can't dismiss that as lightly as people are inclined to.

This morning, the same cool but courteous voice places the order. A dozen long-stemmed roses to Medford Arms on Ninety-first Street. Suite 712. Afternoon delivery. Cash payment will be sent in the mail. If the flowers are accepted, phone this number. If not, throw them away. He'll take his business elsewhere if he finds out the flowers have been sold to another customer. He says goodbye.

"Wait," I say quickly. He's silent on the other end. You can have me, is what I really want to tell him. You can have me, body and soul. Instead I say, "I have something to ask you."

"No, you don't," the man says and hangs up.

Well, I don't blame him. Why should he want to talk to me? He doesn't know that I could give him more than he could ever hope to have with her. I could mend his broken heart.

The reason I know so much about broken hearts is because of Howard and what I did to him. The man's voice has blue written all over it. Grey-blue like the rain, like the hint of colour in the display windows of the shop. I wonder if they're tinted or if it's just the reflection of the bank across the street? The building has some kind of blue tiles on the outside of it. The cars passing make shadows on the surface of the building and turn it into an ocean complete with surf. A city bus shakes the pavement and creates a tidal wave.

Mrs. Boyle comes from the back room where she and Dennis

have been busy looking over inventory lists. She's going to stay on for a month after Dennis takes over, but she wants to have everything in perfect order when she leaves. She asks me why I haven't gone for lunch yet.

Lunch. I look at the clock and realize I've been standing with the telephone receiver in my hand for fifteen minutes, ever since the flower man hung up. I quickly put the phone back on the hook and zip out the front door.

I didn't bring an umbrella this morning, but I like the rain. I decide to walk around for half an hour. Who cares if I look like a wet cocker spaniel. Mrs. Boyle won't say anything, not today she won't. She knows I'm upset about not getting the job. At least she thinks I'm upset. I'm not really. I don't care. I might even quit. I might quit, track down Howard and move back in with him. That would show everyone.

It takes time to figure things out. I'm not going to quit and I'm not going back to Howard. A week of thinking about it has reminded me that I left Howard for a reason. Not a very good one, maybe, but a reason nonetheless. I'm guilty, sure, but that's not going to make things any better. I'm no salesman's wife. And Howard is never going to give up selling to sail around the world with me on a freighter. Broken heart or no broken heart, he's going to have to live without me.

I've thought about this job thing over the past week and I feel much better. Dennis starts his new job next Monday and I know what will happen. He won't be able to do it. They'll have to make him delivery boy again and they'll see that I'm the one they should have given the job to in the first place.

I must have been really upset without knowing it. Imagine me thinking I could move back in with Howard. People get crazy ideas when they're upset about something. I don't look so terrible either. That young cop must have been trying to warn me in a sort of off-hand way. He didn't want to insult Mrs. Boyle by telling me to be especially careful because I was just as pretty as Lila. You can't say things like that when there's another person who is obviously flawed standing right there.

It's a nice sunny morning and I've decided to get off the train two stops before I usually get off. That gives me about a half-hour walk to the flower shop. I left my apartment early so I'd have time to poke along, looking at things, listening to sounds.

I do that a lot. I make up stories about people I see, what's happening in their lives, what's going on behind those doors and windows, who's in control. Of course you can only imagine so much, only what you know yourself. Things might be completely different from what they seem to me.

I can see a woman right now, hanging out of a third-storey apartment window. There's a clothesline in front of her and a basket of clothes on the fire escape. She's screaming. Quite a few people have stopped to stare. Someone must have stolen the clothes from her line. Yes, that's it. She set out a second basket of clothes to hang, then noticed the first had disappeared. Someone stole her clothes, for God's sake. There are people in this world with no morals, no compassion. How do you deal with people like that? It has me beat. This poor woman desperately needs something from that first basket of clothes. Her baby's christening outfit. It's been in the family for years and her baby's supposed to be christened next Sunday and now the little white dress is gone. Things will never be the same for her. And there's nothing any of us can do. No need for any of us to interfere. It won't do any good. There's nothing to be said.

I walk on, really ticked off about what happened back there. Why her? Why, today of all days, would someone steal her baby clothes? I'm so mad I don't know if I'll be able to work. The day started okay because I figured out Dennis is going to lose that job before he hardly gets going. Now I'm just another pair of shoes walking down the sidewalk. In fact, I feel like the sidewalk is pushing me along, stopping me at the red lights, giving me friendly but firm nudges when the lights change. What the subway graffiti says is true. Life sucks and then you die. Some sidewalk pushes you along for fifty or sixty years, then gives you a shove into that big hole in the ground.

A taxi cruises slowly up the street past me. The driver is wearing reflector sunglasses and a cap, has his window rolled down and his arm hanging out. I notice a pack of cigarettes tucked into the rolled-up sleeve of his T-shirt. He stares at me, almost hits a parked car because he's staring. It's a really close call. Why is he staring at me? Maybe he recognizes me from the flower shop. He bought flowers once for his girl friend or his mother. Or maybe it's the young cop. That's it. It's the young cop in disguise. He's looking for Lila's killer. He's following me because he's worried about me. Whoever killed Lila might be after me too. He might have come into the flower shop and seen both Lila and me. He might be watching my apartment, waiting to get me alone somewhere. Good thing I got off the train when I did. The last stop before the shop is a lonely one. Hardly anyone gets off and there's a tunnel you have to walk through to get out of the station. I should probably start getting off at a different stop every day. Randomly selected. A little shiver runs through me, but I feel better about life because it seems I did something right this morning, getting off the train when I did.

When I get to work I immediately begin filling the card trays on the counter by the till. *Best Wishes on Your Retirement. Deepest Sympathy. For a Dear Friend.* No standing around this morning. I feel strangely energetic.

An hour later, the taxi driver starts to nag me again. It's not the business about the killer, that's too far-fetched. There was something familiar about him though, more familiar than a customer would have been, more familiar than the young cop. About noon it hits me. The taxi driver looked an awful lot like Howard. Not that I'd ever seen Howard with reflector sunglasses on, or any sunglasses at all for that matter, but there are some things you can't hide. An aura, I suppose. Yes, the more I think about it, the more I think the taxi driver could have been Howard. By two o'clock, I'm convinced. The taxi driver was Howard, no doubt about it. Howard in disguise. Howard looking out for me because somehow he's heard about Lila being killed. Somehow he's made the connection between Lila and me. Maybe he's known where I was all along and he stays just a little ways behind me. Looking out for me.

Well, this is great. Just great. The first thing that goddamned Dennis does when he gets to be manager is fire me. I can't believe it. I'm sitting here in my apartment, having just been "let go", and I pick up last night's paper and see this job ad: *Sales and delivery personnel wanted for flower shop. Experience required. Apply in person.* He obviously had this planned. The ad doesn't say *chance for advancement* this time. Dennis, God damn him, must be planning to stay for a while.

I cut the ad out of the paper and pin it to the bull's-eye of my dart board. I have it hanging on the wall directly across from the couch so I can throw darts while I'm watching TV.

I'm a pretty good shot and there aren't very many holes in the wall. I'm just about to throw a few when the doorbell rings.

Damn. I don't want to talk to anyone, unless it's Dennis coming to tell me he's changed his mind. Or Howard, but I think I might have been mistaken about Howard in the taxi. I haven't seen him since. I've been watching for him and I haven't seen a thing. Not a goddamned thing.

"Who is it?" I shout, just in case.

"Lila's sister," a voice says through the door. "The Lila you used to work with."

Lila's sister? I didn't know Lila had a sister. What could she want with me? I consider going out the window and down the fire escape, but decide that wouldn't look very good. I should talk to her. I don't have to tell her I hated Lila. She probably won't ask me if I liked Lila. Why would she come here to ask me that? If she doesn't ask I won't say anything. I open the door.

A very overweight woman vaguely resembling Lila stands in the hallway. She's wearing a red poplin tent coat, the kind that's supposed to cover everything but never quite does.

"Lila would have wanted you to have these," she says, shoving a plastic clothes bag at me. "They don't fit me."

It seems like such an understatement I'm not sure what to say next. I sure as hell don't want Lila's clothes. I don't want any dead person's clothes and especially not Lila's.

"Maybe they'll fit you someday," I stammer. "You never know."

"I've been on a diet since I was eight years old," Lila's sister says. "I just keep getting fatter."

I reach out and take the clothes bag. It's too embarrassing, talking on such an intimate level with someone I've never met before. Something tells me I should invite her in, but I can't bear the thought of any further exchange.

She seems to sense this and leaves quickly. I haven't had to tell her I hated Lila. I didn't even have to say thank you for the clothes, which would have been dishonest because I don't want them.

The clothes, of course, are Lila's expensive suits. And her damned fake fingernails are in one of the pockets. Somehow, she planned this. It's like I'm the beneficiary of her will or something, and that gives me more than one motive for killing her.

THE WEDNESDAY FLOWER MAN

Everybody knows when you figure out the motive you've got the killer. Thank God for dumb cops. Still, I stick the fingernails in the sugar bowl and shove the suits down behind the couch in case they come.

It's the last Tuesday of the month again. The flower man will be calling the shop tomorrow morning. I wonder who will take his order, whether or not the man will recognize a different voice, ask about me. I wonder if the new delivery boy will follow the man's orders the way Dennis did, or if he'll simply throw the flowers into the first garbage bin he comes to. Surely he'll ring the apartment doorbell this one time at least. My plan depends on him ringing the doorbell.

I watch the clock all day, waiting for the cover of darkness. I've already checked out the balconies and climbing seven of them shouldn't be difficult as long as no one sees me. I should be able to stand on each one and shinny up to the next level. This will be fairly drastic action, I know, but I see no other way. I did try to figure out the flower man's address by going through the metropolitan area phone book entry by entry, searching for his number (which I have memorized), but I came to the conclusion it's unlisted. Break and enter, I figure, is the only way. If I get caught, I get caught.

Time passes so damned slowly when you have a plan. I don't know what to do with myself. I stare at Lila's suits. They're on the armchair where I piled them after I dug them out from behind the couch, kicking myself for that ridiculous attack of paranoia. As if the police would bother with me.

What do you wear with an expensive suit? Lila always wore light-coloured blouses, pure silk is my guess. I don't have anything like that. I do have a fancy black T-shirt with see-through lace around the neck. That would do for just trying on. Trying on is as far as this will go anyway. I'm sure as hell not planning to wear Lila's suits out in public. This is just to pass the time until tonight. When I look in the mirror it hits me that Lila's pink suit is a pretty damned good disguise.

It's Wednesday, just before noon, about the time the man phones the flower shop. The apartment is empty, just as the caretaker said. I've been here since four o'clock in the morning, having successfully picked the lock on the sliding patio doors.

I'm glad my apartment doesn't have them. I've just proven any amateur can break in that way.

I limp around, favouring the knee I banged climbing over every one of the seven balconies. I look for clues. A hair on the carpet. A chip of a fingernail. A trace of perfume or hair spray in the air. Nothing. I find nothing to put together a picture of the flower man's lady friend. Until I get to the bathroom, where I find a gold mine in the medicine cabinet. She must have forgotten about it. Did I forget about the medicine cabinet when I left Howard? I wouldn't have left anything very interesting anyway. A box of Tampax and a toothbrush maybe. But this woman, she must have been a walking cosmetic counter. Makeup, cleansing creams, moisturizers, deodorant, shampoo, hair conditioner. You name it. Even hair dye. Brandy wine, whatever colour that might be. Sounds vaguely purple.

Hair dye. I look at my watch and figure there's another hour anyway before the flowers arrive.

The water's still hooked up. I bend over the sink, wet my hair and dab the gooey dye all over. I make the mistake of standing up to look in the mirror and it drips down my face and onto Lila's suit. Shit. I want a disguise, not a Hallowe'en costume. I do my best to wring my hair out over the sink, then sit on the plush carpet by the fireplace to wait for the doorbell. I think about the time I dyed my hair to hide from Howard. I did it in the washroom at the airport, then dried it under the hand dryer. I wish I had a dryer now. The apartment is warm enough, but my wet hair makes me shiver.

The roses will be in a long box with a gold ribbon tied around it. No need to unwrap it. I already know what will be inside. Twelve long-stemmed with assorted greenery. A few of the blooms will be past their prime and I'll blame that on Dennis' mismanagement. He'll have figured they're just going to get thrown out. Little does he know. If I were manager I would never send shoddy roses. The man's a regular customer. He has a broken heart. He should get the best.

I wish I could see the look on Dennis' face when the new delivery boy tells him someone answered the door. I was originally planning to hide behind the door so Dennis couldn't figure out it was me from the kid's description. But now I don't think I'll bother. With Lila's pink wool suit and brandy wine hair I don't think I have to worry. Dennis will never in a million years think it was me. Lila come back from the dead, maybe, but not me.

I imagine that I have the box of roses in my arms.

"Ah, Howard," I say out loud. "You always were a romantic son-of-a-bitch." Then I laugh. It would have been fun to say that to Howard.

Try this. "Howie, Howie, Howie. I knew you'd find me some day. (Sigh) Where do we go from here?"

Sounds funny. Maybe it's the empty apartment. The acoustics are off.

I wonder if the Wednesday flower man will come after the roses are delivered. Yes, of course he will. Why else has he left instructions for contacting him? He will come, that's certain.

But what then? What if the goings on behind this closed door were other than what I supposed? My scenario, of course, has been that he will be disappointed that I'm not her, but glad all the same to have an understanding someone to talk to. And from there, who knows? Dinner. A movie. His place. A private yacht. Europe.

But as I sit here on the floor with the roses, other scenarios, moving pictures, begin to play on the wall across the room. The man is not a stranger after all, but someone I've seen before. A taxi driver passing slowly. A young policeman in disguise. A killer. Howard. I close my eyes to make the pictures go away, but they're inside my head. I open them again and see the red roses, red fingernails. Close. Open. Open. Close. It's hypnotizing, like someone swinging a watch on a chain in front of your eyes. Maybe it's because I was up all night, making my way up the balconies, wondering if the flowers would come. I doze off.

The doorbell. It rings and I jump to my feet and try to straighten up my hair. It's dry except for the side I was sleeping on. I hope the dye didn't leave any stains on my forehead and I pull my bangs down, using my fingers as a comb. No time to run to the bathroom and check to see how I look. However I look, it will have to do.

The ringing stops. I hurry to the door and open it in time to see a delivery boy throwing a box of flowers down the chute in the hallway. "Wait," I start to say, but he is already disappearing around a corner, disappearing so quickly I don't even see what he looks like. "Wait," I whisper, but he's gone. No flowers, no flower man.

What to do. Run after the delivery boy? Call the flower man

39

myself and say the roses were delivered? Wait another month for another box of roses? What should I do? What would be best?

None of the above. It's a dark hour, I think, as I limp down the stairwell, a dark hour indeed. I leave the stained pink suit jacket hanging on the banister at the foot of the stairs and walk home.

Saturday morning. I've spent the last two days holed up in my apartment looking at the rest of Lila's suits. Then I woke up this morning and for some strange reason I wanted to go back to the flower shop. I don't want to go inside, but I'd kind of like to sneak a peek in the window, maybe see Dennis making a mess of everything.

It's pouring rain again, so I carry my umbrella. I take Lila's suits with me too, in a green garbage bag, and dump them into the Sally Ann drop-box just around the corner from the flower shop. After that's done I feel free. Her fingernails are still in my sugar bowl, but I might leave them there for a little remembrance.

No slow-cruising taxis today. They're all busy, going somewhere with a purpose, just like me. As I approach the shop, I see them, Dennis and Mrs. Boyle, in the big plate glass display window, staring out at the rain. They look sad. They probably miss me. They're probably sorry about what they've done to me. Well, it's too late now. I do have a certain amount of pride.

There's a man across the street, up against the blue tile building, shaking the rain off his coat. He doesn't have an umbrella. I duck under an awning and stare at him. He begins to look familiar. If I didn't know better, I'd think it was Howard. He's fumbling in his pocket, pulling something out. Orange and green slips of paper the size of a business envelope. He looks across the street at me. He waves the papers in the air, waves them right at me, not caring if they get wet. It is Howard. Howard with two freighter tickets to Singapore. I cross the street without even a glance at the flower shop. Good old Howard. He'll be so happy to have me back.

SUNDAY RODEOS

Through the fence I can see him riding around the arena on that big black horse of his. They aren't all here yet, all the cowboys, and he is just riding around, coiling up his rope and tossing it out real gentle, not like he means to catch anything at all. He comes up here every Sunday afternoon with the other cowboys and sometimes he gets here early. He might be coming to see me, I think. He might. He knows I'm watching him right now, even though I try to look like I'm doing something else. Like maybe wiping the dust off my new boots that Mr. and Mrs. Olsen bought me. Or maybe drawing pictures in the dirt with a stick. "You stay away from the men," Mrs. Olsen always tells me. "You can go up there to watch but be sure to keep out of the road."

I do keep out of the road. I don't want to get sent away from here. I've been sent to a lot of different places and I like this one best. Mr. and Mrs. Olsen don't try to get you to call them Mom and Dad like some people do.

He rides up here every Sunday on that black horse. His wife Loretta doesn't ever come with him. She's too scared he'll get hurt, I heard them say, she's too chicken to watch. I'm not. I like it when they almost get hurt. It makes your heart beat a little bit fast and it makes me think if he was my man I would run right out there and I would say "oh baby are you all right" and he would say "yeah darlin' I'm okay" and he would maybe lean on me just a tiny bit and all the people would clap for him because they would know that really he is hurting bad.

He's riding by so close I can hear his big horse breathing. I don't look up. I just keep on drawing in the dirt. I draw a big heart and put an arrow through it. When he has gone by, I put

41

my initials and his inside the heart. I look at it, then scratch it out real fast.

I've seen Loretta in town a few times. She's got a skinny waist and big tits and that's probably why he married her because she doesn't have anything else, at least not that I can see. She has a funny nose, a real honker, and she's got this laugh that would drive you crazy if you had to be around her. I would tell her to shut up, just shut up that stupid mouth. I might even hit her if she didn't do what I said. I probably would hit her because she would drive me crazy.

One by one the other cowboys come and they herd the stock into the corral at one end of the arena. The stock is Mr. Olsen's and that's why they come here every Sunday, because he's got rodeo stock and this arena. Those cows run by me and kick up a lot of dust and the calves bawl and then they're all milling around in a circle. If I was Loretta I would be here to shut the gate. I would do it at just the right time and no one would have to tell me when. He would be thinking what a good job I did. If he was married to me I sure as hell wouldn't stay home from Sunday rodeos and miss all the fun.

I like to watch from the far end of the arena where the cowboys go when they're finished their ride. They sit on the fence sometimes with their horses tied to the rails and they talk about what kind of ride they had and how tough that calf was or how they should eat the goddamned thing for supper because as soon as it felt the rope it just lay down. They don't like those ones. They like the ones that give them a good fight even if it does take longer and then their time isn't so good. If they figure out one calf is harder to get down, everyone wants it.

Sometimes they save the easy ones for the young guys, the ones who are my age. I don't like to watch them. They're always so proud of themselves when they manage to get the rope on and they stand in the arena and grin like they're waiting for a medal or something. And they always walk by me just to show off and if one of them ever says anything to me like "hey girl you want to go for a walk over to those bushes" I will say "not with you zit-face." He won't tell Mr. Olsen either, because he would know they were talking to me and he's probably told them to stay away. They're trying real hard to keep me out of trouble but they don't have to worry. I'm not going to do anything stupid so I get sent away from this place. I love these Sunday rodeos so much they are better than Christmas.

In the middle of the afternoon they all go up to the house for lunch and I have to go early to help Mrs. Olsen make sandwiches and cut up cake into squares. Some of the wives come up to the house too and sometimes they bring cake and cookies and other stuff with them. Not Loretta though, she never sends anything.

Mrs. Olsen's got one of those coffee pots that holds about a hundred cups and she sets out a bunch of basins with hot water at the side of the house so the men can wash up before they sit down to lunch. Mr. and Mrs. Olsen have a real nice yard with lots of grass and flowers and they have picnic tables just like in a park. When the men are washing up I hide around the corner and watch to see which basin he uses. After they are all sitting down I go and look at the water and the grey scum floating on top. If no one is watching I rub soap all over my face and arms right up to my elbows, just the way he does. Then I splash that dirty water all over and rub myself with a towel until my skin turns pink. One time Mr. Olsen saw me doing that and he laughed. I ran and hid in the hayloft where it's soft and smells good, and I didn't even help with the dishes and I said fuck you five times for everyone I could think of. Except *him*. I stayed there until after supper and then I sneaked into the house and went to my bedroom and got into bed. They came looking for me but I pretended to be asleep and they didn't try to wake me. They just closed the door real quiet and I heard the boards squeaking as they tip-toed down the hall. After that I got out of bed and sat in the window for a long time. In the dark, you can see the lights of his place way down the road, his and Loretta's. Sometimes I look down there and wonder what they're doing and I just hate that bitch because I know she's on top of him right now, screwing him for all she's worth. Once, when there was a big moon in the sky, I took all my clothes off and sat in the window and let the moon shine in on me. I thought if he was looking out the window he would maybe be able to see me and then he would tell Loretta where to go and she would have to do without, at least for one night.

Today there are too many people and I can't wash up in the basins. I have to go to the washroom in the house. I stay in there for a while, then I go outside and start gathering up the

43

cups. Mrs. Olsen looks surprised like she's seen a ghost, then she smiles and I know I've done the right thing. I carry the cups to the kitchen to wash them, but I do it too fast and break one and I think what's one stupid cup anyway, they've got so many cups I could break a dozen and they'd never know the difference. Just the same, I hide the broken cup way at the back of the cupboard.

After lunch is over with, the cowboys get down to the stuff I really like to watch. I love it when they wrestle those steers to the ground. And you can tell they love it too because about then they get the coolers filled with beer out of the trucks and they swear more and tell good stories about guys getting hurt.

What they do is this. Two cowboys ride out together after they let a steer out of the chute. One cowboy keeps him going in a straight line while the other one leans down from the saddle and grabs the steer around the neck. The horses are running real fast and when the cowboy's got the steer just right he slides off his horse and twists that steer's neck until you think it's going to break and that's how he wrestles him to the ground. All this happens real fast and you have to watch every minute if you want to see the exciting part, right when the cowboy slides down into the dirt and almost gets his guts stepped on.

After they've finished their ride they walk back to the end of the arena away from the chutes and someone might open a beer and by now they are really dirty. The sweat bands on their hats make a ring across their foreheads and you can see it when they take their hats off to wipe at the sweat with their shirt sleeves. They don't swear if they know I'm around so I sneak along the fence and crouch down real low.

That's where I am, crouched down, listening, when he rides up behind me on that big black horse. And my heart starts pounding like there's something wrong with me and I might die and he says, "You ever been on a horse?" I wipe the dust off my brand new boots with my hands and stand up real tall like I'm proud I've never been on a horse before, even though I'm scared and I hide whenever Mr. Olsen saddles up his old nag and says he's going to teach me how to ride. I shake my head and he leans down and holds out his hand. He kicks his foot out of the stirrup and I put mine in like I've seen them do a hundred times and he lifts me up behind him as if I don't weigh anything at all. I put my arms around his waist and I can tell that he is all muscle, not a bit of fat on him, and he has the reins in one hand, a beer in the other and we ride around outside the arena. When he asks if I've had enough I shake my head and point to the arena and he turns his horse and heads in there without even blinking. They are about to let another steer out of the chute and two cowboys are ready to ride, but he holds up his hand and tells them to wait. We ride all the way around the arena and some of the cowboys clap and cheer and I can tell Mr. Olsen isn't mad. Then we head over to the fence and I climb off onto the rails and I stay on the fence, up on the top rail where everyone can see me.

I can see real good from the fence, and so I see it all when he goes for a big steer and something happens and he's under the steer and its hooves go onto his chest and stomach and he rolls like a stuffed doll, then lies there quiet on the ground right in front of me.

I want to go to him and hold his head on my lap and call him baby but I don't move. People are crowding around him and he is moving now, throwing up in the dirt, holding his stomach, doubled up like he hurts so bad and it almost makes me cry. "We gotta take him into town," someone says, but he shakes his head and says he's not going. Some cowboys help him outside the arena and he lies down on the grass with his knees pulled up to his chest. I get down off the fence and hide around the corner again so I can see what's going on. "You ought to go into town," someone says to him, but he closes his eyes and says he'll be all right as soon as he gets his wind back. I can see real good through the fence rails and his shirt is undone and there's blood on his chest where the steer stepped on him. "Someone better go call Loretta," one guy says. "He won't listen to us." Someone else leads the black horse out of the arena and ties her to a fence rail.

After a bit he seems to breathe better and pretty soon he puts his legs down and doesn't look like he hurts so much. Some cowboys are sitting on the ground around him, some of them have beer, and pretty soon one guy says that was the god-damnedest fall he ever saw anybody take and still come up alive and somebody else tells a story about how once he saw a guy with a hole right through his stomach and another guy had a broken neck and died on the way to the hospital. Some of the cowboys get back on their horses and the action in the arena starts up again.

By the time Loretta gets here he's leaning kind of funny against the fence rails, drinking a beer. Loretta drives up real fast and slams the door of the truck when she gets out. You can tell she's mad but he just grins at her and she calls him a crazy goddamned fool. Not darling or baby or sweetheart. Just a goddamned fool. "I'm taking you to the hospital," she says, and he says he guesses he'll go because he thinks he has a busted rib or two. He tips his head back and drains the bottle, then he sees me all crouched down in the grass. "Hey," he calls and motions with his arm for me to come over. This time I don't stand up quite so tall because Loretta's there and she's looking at me over that big honker of hers. But I go just the same. "You think you can lead this horse down to the barn?" he says to me. "She's real gentle." I haven't led a horse anywhere before and I'm scared but I nod my head anyway. He shows me how easy it is to take off the saddle and bridle and tells me to give her a drink and turn her loose in the corral in front of the barn. He undoes the reins and hands them to me. "Tell Olsen I'll be over for her later," he says. Loretta holds out her arm for him but he won't take it. He walks pretty stiff to the truck and climbs in onthe passenger side. I see him lay his head on the back of the seat and Loretta gets in and they are gone.

"Want me to take her?" one of the cowboys asks and I shake my head and don't look at him and walk toward the barn, praying that horse comes along behind and doesn't walk too fast or try to go somewhere else on me. But she walks just right and I lead her to the water trough where she has a long drink, sucking the water up between her lips, all the time looking at me with those big eyes. When she's done I lead her into the corral and tie her to a fence rail while I undo the cinch around her middle. The saddle's heavy but I know I can do it. It slides down, blanket and all, and I almost fall but I manage to get it to the barn where I put it down in one of the stalls. I go back to that black horse and she even lets me stroke her nose before I slip the bridle off and she feels so soft it makes me cry. I lay my face against her neck and she just stands there like she knows and I'll bet she hates Loretta too and is goddamned glad she doesn't come to Sunday rodeos.

46

THE ELITE CAFE

All the houses on this block are the same, Rachel thought. She was looking out the front window at the row of identical white wartime houses across the street.

It was Saturday morning. Rachel's mother had hauled the washing machine out of the back porch and was doing the wash in the kitchen. Rachel had to stay out of there because there were piles of sorted laundry everywhere and she had seen Jimmy Washington's arm after he put it through the wringer. She didn't believe for a minute he put it through the wringer on purpose, but every time her mother sounded the warning, Rachel had a little flash of fear that she might lose control and feed one of her own arms through the wringer the way her mother fed the sheets. For this reason, she steered clear.

Rachel was waiting for ten o'clock to roll around so she could wander down the block and see who was doing what.

"That's good manners," her mother said. "You don't visit or phone anyone before ten o'clock in the morning."

Good manners and the right way to do things were important to Rachel's mother. Rachel could not for the life of her figure out why.

From the front window, Rachel could see Mrs. Rogoza on her way to work at the Elite Cafe. She was wearing bright blue high-heeled shoes. Rachel waved at her and was surprised, a little hurt even, that Mrs. Rogoza didn't wave back.

Of course Rachel had no way of knowing what Mrs. Rogoza was thinking, no way of knowing that she was planning to stop at the cafe for her cheque, then catch the 10:45 bus as far east as it would take her. There were other cafes, Mrs. Rogoza was thinking. All across the country there were cafes crying out for

47

waitresses with her experience. She was not thinking about Melanie or Petie or Mr. Rogoza. She saw Rachel in her front window as she walked by, but she didn't think about her either. She looked right through Rachel's house as though it didn't exist.

Mrs. Rogoza didn't know it, but Rachel was her greatest admirer. Rachel loved her dyed red hair pulled back and pinned in a French roll. She loved her white waitresses' uniform with its walking slit in the back. She loved her false fingernails. Rachel had watched her glue them on once. Mrs. Rogoza had been sitting at the kitchen table in her slip.

"The light is better here," she had explained to Rachel.

When Rachel saw Mrs. Rogoza walking to work in her blue high-heeled shoes, she supposed the little suitcase in her hand contained another pair. Rachel's mother always took a change of shoes with her.

"You've got to take care of your feet," she told Rachel often. She bought Rachel's shoes a full size too big just to make sure they weren't too small.

Rachel's mother came into the room and stood behind her in the window.

"I think Mrs. Rogoza is more beautiful than the Queen," Rachel said.

"There's something odd about her," Rachel's mother said. What she was thinking was that Mrs. Rogoza wore too much makeup and seemed to take more of an interest in her personal appearance than she did in her children. More than once Melanie had come to play wearing her pyjama top from the night before.

Rachel was worried about her mother's tone of voice. It would be just like her to say she couldn't play at the Rogozas' anymore. Rachel had been careful not to let slip that sometimes there wasn't any babysitter at the Rogozas'. Now she wondered if maybe her mother had somehow found out about the time she and Melanie hid in the bushes in the Rogozas' front yard and yelled "Dirty Diapers to the King" at everyone who walked by the house.

"I used to think the Queen was more beautiful than Elizabeth Taylor," Rachel said, "but now I think Mrs. Rogoza is more beautiful than both of them." Rachel knew her mother thought Elizabeth Taylor was the most beautiful woman in the world. She had read bits of a magazine article aloud to Rachel once, a survey of hundreds of people who had been asked their opinion on who was the most beautiful woman in the world. Elizabeth Taylor had won, hands down.

"Well," Rachel's mother said, "Melanie seems like a nice enough girl." Not too silly, not too wild, she thought. And she certainly looked out for her little brother. That was nice to see.

"Is it ten o'clock yet?" Rachel asked.

"No," her mother said, "but I guess you can go out and play anyway. Just stay on the block." Rachel bolted out the front door and headed up the street to the Rogozas'.

Mr. Rogoza was sitting on the back step in his undershirt drinking a beer. He ignored Rachel as she stepped quickly past him and went on into the house. He wasn't thinking about anything. He tried hard not to think. He didn't know his wife was about to catch a bus to parts unknown, but if he had he would have tried not to think about it.

Melanie was in the bathroom giving Petie a bath.

"Do you think your father would let us play with the box?" Rachel asked Melanie as she was lifting Petie out of the tub. He was squealing because he had soap in his eyes.

"I don't know," Melanie answered. "He's kind of grouchy. He's been sitting there all morning. Maybe even all last night."

Rachel heard Mr. Rogoza open the screen door.

"I'm going out for a while," he hollered. "You watch your little brother, you hear?"

"He's supposed to stay home with us," Melanie said, rubbing Petie's wet hair with a faded beach towel. "But I don't care if he goes out. Doesn't make a bit of difference to me."

"Did you hear what I said?" Mr. Rogoza hollered from the back door.

"Course I did," Melanie snapped. Rachel marvelled at her haughtiness. The screen door slammed again.

"Maybe he's going to find a new job," Rachel suggested.

"Yeah, probably," Melanie said. "But I don't care. My mom has a real good job. That cafe couldn't run without her. Nobody but my mom knows what they're doing. I wouldn't be surprised if she buys it."

"Buys the cafe?" Rachel was amazed. Could Mrs. Rogoza really buy the Elite Cafe? She could just see herself and Melanie working there when they were old enough, serving pie and ice cream in their white uniforms and high-heeled shoes.

"Yeah," Melanie said. "The guy that owns it now is a complete idiot. My mom said so."

Rachel had been inside the Elite Cafe only once. She and Melanie had walked downtown without telling anyone because they'd heard on the radio you could get free ladies' gloves for Mother's Day at the Five and Dime. When they got there, they found out you had to buy ten dollars worth of stuff before you got the gloves, so they'd had to leave empty-handed. They hung around for a while outside the Elite Cafe, sneaking peeks at Mrs. Rogoza until she saw them through the big plate glass window. Instead of chasing them home, she hauled them inside and bought them each a Coke. Rachel hadn't told her mother. Downtown cafes were off limits.

Melanie finished dressing Petie and turned him loose.

"Come on," she said to Rachel. "Let's get the box."

The box was a cardboard one from the grocery store. It had *Spic and Span* written on the side in green and yellow letters. Mr. Rogoza had been a Fuller Brush salesman for a brief time and the box was full of things he was to have given people as free gifts. When he lost his job, he had to give the special carrying case back but he had kept the free gifts and dumped them in the Spic and Span carton. Melanie fished it out from under Mr. and Mrs. Rogoza's bed and carried it to the living room. Rachel and Melanie sat side by side on the linoleum and examined the contents.

Rachel particularly liked the miniature tubes of lipstick. They were like jewels in a sea of pocket combs and plastic kitchen gadgets. Spitfire Red was the best. That was the colour Mrs. Rogoza wore.

"You can pick one," Melanie said, "but the Spitfire Reds are gone. My mom took them all before she went to work this morning."

Melanie had stood in the bedroom doorway and watched her mother picking through the box, tossing all the little tubes of lipstick into her suitcase.

"Don't stare," her mother had said to her. "Didn't anyone teach you it's not polite to stare?"

Rachel chose a tube with *Oriole Orange* written on the bottom. She took the lid off and felt the smooth oily surface with her finger. She didn't dare put it on her lips. Her mother would have a fit.

Rachel thought it was too bad for Mrs. Rogoza that Mr. Rogoza wasn't a Fuller Brush man anymore. Sooner or later, the little tubes of Spitfire Red were bound to run out.

"Let's play Fuller Brush man," Rachel said. "We haven't been to the Marcotte's yet."

"I have to watch Petie," Melanie said.

"That doesn't matter," said Rachel. "Say he's your little boy. Say your wife is at work and you have to take him with you door to door."

"I guess that would be okay," Melanie said. Her dad had taken her with him once. She'd been disgusted. He hadn't sold a thing all day.

They got Petie from the back yard, then carried the box to the Marcotte's house. Petie hid behind Melanie as she rang the doorbell.

"Hello," said Melanie when Mrs. Marcotte answered the door. "I'm selling Fuller Brush products. Would you like to choose a free gift from this box?"

Mrs. Marcotte eyed them suspiciously. "Does your father know you're doing this?" she asked.

"Of course he does," Melanie said. "He asked us to do it for him."

Rachel felt something strange coming over her. She knew she should be careful what she said in front of Mrs. Marcotte, but she couldn't help herself.

"He asked us to do it because we're so good at it," Rachel said. "He lost his job because he couldn't sell enough stuff."

Melanie looked at her viciously. Rachel was taken off guard by this. She thought Melanie was going to throw the box at her, then Melanie turned back to Mrs. Marcotte and smiled politely, just like a good salesman should.

"Well, I don't think I need anything today," Mrs. Marcotte said. She was surprised by Rachel's shameless behaviour. Her mother would want to know about this door-to-door business.

That little Melanie was a different story altogether. Poor Mrs. Rogoza, Mrs. Marcotte thought. She had brought things upon herself, no doubt. But still, one couldn't help feeling sorry. Melanie was probably going to turn out just like her. Rachel should be told not to hang around the Rogozas. Rachel noticed the very pointed look Mrs. Marcotte gave her before she closed the door.

"What did you say that for?" Melanie hissed at Rachel as they headed down the Marcotte's front step with Petie in tow.

"It's true, isn't it?" said Rachel.

"Well, you don't have to tell everyone."

Rachel felt a pang of remorse. "It doesn't matter," she said, trying to make things all right again. "Your mom has the best job in the world. I wish my mom worked at the Elite Cafe."

"I guess we should put this away," Melanie said, looking at the box. "My dad might come home."

They carried the box back to the bedroom and Melanie shoved it under the bed. Rachel looked at the wedding picture of Mr. and Mrs. Rogoza on the dresser.

"Do you think my mom's pretty?" Melanie asked Rachel.

"Yes," Rachel answered. "Don't you?"

"I don't know if she is or not," said Melanie. "Mostly I think she is, but sometimes my dad tells her she looks like hell. Then I look at her and I think she does."

"I don't care what your dad says," Rachel said. "I think your mom is beautiful. If she decides not to buy the Elite Cafe, I bet she could be a movie star."

The bedroom window was open and Rachel could hear her own mother calling her. She ran up the alley and passed Mr. Currie in his back yard, working at his forge. He was an inventor. Hidden under the mattress of her bed, Rachel had a fluorescent lead ball that Mr. Currie had invented for exercising your eyes. You dangled it on a string in the dark and followed the movement back and forth without turning your head. Mark Currie had handed them out to all the kids in the neighbourhood. Sometimes at night Rachel exercised her eyes before she went to sleep.

When Rachel got into the house, the phone was ringing. She answered it.

"Hello, Rachel," a voice said. "I would like to speak to your mother, if I may." Rachel recognized the voice.

"I'm very sorry," Rachel said, "but my mother is not home just now. Would you like her to call you?"

"Yes, Rachel," the voice said. "I would like her to call Mrs. Marcotte."

Rachel hung up the phone.

"Who was that?" her mother asked when she came back from wheeling the washing machine into the porch.

"Nobody," Rachel said. "Wrong number, I guess. They wanted to speak to someone named Alexandria Whittingham."

"My goodness," Rachel's mother said. "Who in this town could have a name like that?"

After lunch, Rachel and her mother walked downtown to do some shopping. They passed the Elite Cafe and Rachel peered in the window, trying to get a glimpse of Mrs. Rogoza. Her mother pulled her away.

"Quit your dilly-dallying," she said impatiently.

The truth of it was, she did not want to see her neighbour, Mrs. Rogoza, worked off her feet, sweating, harassed by strange men. There was a sign in the window, *Waitress Wanted*, and she shuddered to think of the poor woman who would have to take that thankless job. It was better to stay home and keep your house clean and your family in line, she thought. Even young single girls should not have to work in cafes. They should be encouraged to take some kind of training; a typing course would get them further than working in a cafe. She would encourage Rachel to take a one-year course somewhere. She might work for just a few years before getting married, but it would be some place respectable.

"Can we go in there for a Coke?" Rachel asked.

"Certainly not," her mother said.

Rachel sulked the whole time they were downtown. When her mother, modelling in front of the department store mirror, asked how Rachel thought she looked in a brown cloth coat, Rachel said, "Awful."

It was almost Rachel's bedtime when Melanie knocked on the front door. She wanted to know how to make hamburgers.

"My mom didn't come home from work this afternoon so I guess I should make Petie some supper," she said.

"Is your father home?" Rachel's mother asked, concerned.

"Yeah, but he can't cook anything," said Melanie. "Anyway, I found some hamburger meat in the fridge and Petie likes hamburgers."

Rachel's mother told Melanie how to make hamburgers. She wrote it down on a piece of paper so Melanie wouldn't forget.

"If you want it to go farther," she told her, "you add an egg or two and some oatmeal."

Then Melanie went home to make supper for Petie and her father. Petie burnt his mouth because he bit into his hamburger when it was too hot. Melanie hugged him until he stopped crying.

Mr. Rogoza sat at the table and ate his hamburger as though Melanie and Petie weren't there. He was trying not to think about them. Eventually, he knew, he would have to, but for now he thought about his hamburger. He took big bites and then washed them down with beer. He liked the feel of the cold beer bottle on his lips. Petie's crying was far away, as if it was coming from the neighbour's TV set.

As Rachel lay in the dark that night, she exercised her eyes with Mr. Currie's fluorescent lead ball. It reminded her of Mrs. Rogoza, something beautiful out there in the night.

The next morning, after Rachel came home from Sunday school, Melanie came to the door again. She had the box with her. She wanted Rachel's mother.

"Did your mother come home last night?" Rachel's mother asked Melanie.

Melanie shook her head. "My dad called the police this morning," she said. "I guess she ran away again."

"Where do you think she went?" Rachel's mother asked, touching the top of Melanie's head gently. Melanie ducked and came up free of the hand. She shrugged.

"I don't know," she said. "Last time she went to Winnipeg."

Rachel and her mother were quiet. Rachel's mother didn't know what to say. What could you say to a little girl whose mother has just walked out on her? It was unthinkable. The woman must be disturbed, she thought. She had known that something was not quite right.

"I asked my dad if you could pick something from the box," Melanie said to Rachel's mother. "He's a Fuller Brush man. At least he used to be."

Rachel watched her mother finger the objects in the box.

"The Spitfire Reds are all gone," said Rachel, "but there are lots of other colours left."

Her mother held up a yellow plastic dish with slits in it.

"I think I'll take this little thing here," she said.

"What's it for?" asked Rachel, disappointed.

"Separating eggs," her mother said. She thanked Melanie and watched her take the box back down the block to her own house, where Mr. Rogoza was sitting by the telephone, waiting.

Rachel sat on the front steps. She wondered where Mrs. Rogoza was. She wondered if she still had her uniform on. And her blue high-heeled shoes. She thought Mrs. Rogoza would probably miss the Elite Cafe, even if she did buy a better one somewhere. She was probably thinking about the Elite Cafe right now.

Mrs. Rogoza was not thinking about the Elite Cafe. She was fixing her makeup in the washroom of Eddie's West Side Esso in Kenora, Ontario, carefully applying Spitfire Red, trying to make her thin lips appear fuller. There was a restaurant in the service station, one with a *Waitress Wanted* sign in the window. Mrs. Rogoza fixed up her eyes as best she could, then tried to smooth the wrinkles out of her uniform. She thought that if any man said she looked like hell now, she would have to agree with him. Crying was the absolutely worst thing for your looks, apart from getting old.

MODERN GIRLS

Bored, Moira leaned on the counter and eyed the case of delicate blown glass in front of her. It was too precarious, she thought. Some convention-drunk businessman was sure to knock over the entire display. She considered moving the glass herself, but was afraid she'd be the one to send it crashing to the floor. Then what would she tell Mrs. Hanna? Better it was the businessman, she decided.

Moira looked out into the plush lobby of the CN Hotel and saw that the day's convention traffic had died down. She glanced at her watch, remembering that she'd arranged to meet Carly for a drink after work. Half an hour yet. She hated this last half-hour of the day, it was always slow, but she told herself not to complain. She'd been lucky to find a job so soon after moving back. She'd stopped in to see old Mrs. Hanna just to say hello and it turned out she was looking for somebody to run her boutique for two months while she went on her world cruise. Moira didn't profess to know much about art or craft, but she did enjoy galleries and had worked in a book store in Vancouver for two years. Mrs. Hanna convinced her she'd do just fine. She promised Moira she'd be back in time to organize everything for the Christmas rush.

"Maybe I won't be Mrs. Hanna anymore," she'd winked.

Moira pictured the cruise as a floating singles club. She thought Mrs. Hanna should be too old for that, but apparently not. Mrs. Hanna certainly seemed clear about what she was doing.

Moira watched as a man, thirty-five or so, stepped from a brass elevator across the lobby and walked toward her. He was tall and attractive. For some reason his aviator glasses reminded Moira of a foreign film. She looked away as he entered the shop

57

and tried not to stare as he perused the rack of Canadian art postcards. He chose a card and carried it to the counter.

"My wife has a collection," the man said, then laughed. "I'll be home before this gets to her, but I always send them through the mail."

Moira was pleased that he told her this, that he appeared so ready to talk about his wife. His voice was warm and casual, his eyes sincere. Lucky wife, Moira thought. She smiled as casually as she could and looked at the postcard he'd chosen.

A work entitled *The Market Garden* was reproduced on the front, a work Moira happened to be familiar with. She explained that the artist, Victor Cicansky, was local. Together Moira and the man looked at the image of an elderly couple, hands touching, surrounded by baskets and crates of brightly coloured garden produce. The idyllic scene was protected by a frame of flowering cucumber vines. Moira had actually seen the original in a local gallery and she told the man it was a ceramic mural in relief. She ran her fingers around the image on the card and described the richness of the glazed vegetables. She was surprised she could talk so easily about the piece. Usually she felt inadequate when she was asked questions about any of the beautiful things Mrs. Hanna had in the shop.

"I'd like to see the original," the man said as he turned the postcard over on the counter and searched his jacket pocket for a pen. Moira looked discreetly away as he began to write.

"I suppose you might be able to track it down," she said.

"I live in Vancouver," the man said. "I'll watch for his name."

It was silly, Moira knew, but when she heard him say Vancouver she wanted to say, "I used to live in Vancouver," and rhyme off a dozen or so names of people she knew there. Actually, there was only one name she wanted to say, but she decided not to because if by chance he did know him she'd have to say "small world" and that really would be silly. Instead, she told him he could leave the postcard if he liked and she'd mail it for him.

"Thank you," the man said, licking a stamp and positioning it carefully, "but I can do that."

His eye was suddenly caught by the case of blown glass.

"It's beautiful, isn't it?" said Moira.

The man agreed and said he thought he would buy a piece, a goblet perhaps.

"Does your wife collect glass as well?" Moira asked, feeling strangely intimate.

The man told her she did indeed, and Moira knew from his tone that he did not think her question too forward. She helped him choose a particularly delicate goblet with an extra-long stem, then wrapped it in tissue and placed it carefully in a box. As she handed it to the man she had the urge to reach up and run her fingers through his thick hair. Horrified that he might read her thoughts, she withdrew quickly and rang up the sale.

"Perhaps you should carry that with you on the plane," Moira called to him as he left the shop. She didn't want anything to happen to the goblet.

She watched him disappear into one of the brass elevators in the lobby, then looked at her watch. She was relieved to see it was six o'clock. As she grabbed her coat, she noticed the man had forgotten the postcard on the counter. She looked at the closed elevator door, then stuck the card in her pocket, planning to drop it in the hotel mail on her way out.

The temperature had dropped. Moira walked quickly, buttoning her coat to the collar, thinking that as soon as the snow started to fly she would probably regret having left Vancouver. She jammed her hands into her pockets and, feeling the postcard, realized she'd forgotten to leave it at the hotel desk.

The Beachport Lounge was several blocks from the hotel and as she walked, Moira wondered why Carly was so fond of the place. She said she loved the plastic pineapples and the lacquered blowfish hanging from the ceiling, but Moira couldn't see it. It was simply tacky as far as she was concerned. And Carly's love of tacky decor seemed like a stupid kind of elitism that she didn't have much patience with. Moira wondered whether these tête-à-têtes with Carly were worthwhile at all because she just found herself getting mad. She was mad already and she wasn't even there yet. Still, Carly was an old friend. She couldn't quit seeing her out of the blue. And she had to admit Carly could be entertaining.

As Moira rounded the corner and saw the Beachport's neon palm tree, she noticed a mailbox across the street. She shivered in the cold wind and decided to run the postcard over on her way home.

"All right, Moira," said Carly boldly just as soon as the drinks were ordered. "I want to hear once and for all about this guy in Vancouver. He was married, wasn't he?"

Moira was not surprised by the question. She knew that Carly, as nosy as she was, had been giving her time to come out with the story on her own. Now her time was up. She should have guessed when Carly called her that morning. Moira looked across the table at her and felt trapped.

"Well?" Carly leaned toward Moira expectantly. "Was he or wasn't he?"

Moira considered denying it, but knew she wasn't a good liar.

"You're annoyingly perceptive," she said to Carly.

"I knew it," Carly said, excited. She leaned back in her chair and tossed her dark hair over her shoulders dramatically. "All single women are attracted to a married man at some point."

Moira was about to tell Carly she didn't know Steve was married until well into their relationship, but decided to let it pass. Carly had had an affair with a married man three years ago and Moira figured she'd been trying to rationalize it ever since. Although Carly had never admitted it, Moira suspected that Carly thought it was morally wrong. It lessened her guilt that Moira had committed the same sin.

"In fact," Carly was saying, "I think every woman should have at least one affair with a married man. Maybe two or three. It matures you, don't you think? I mean, if women are going to live in a modern world they have to be able to handle things."

Moira watched Carly finger a large hoop in her ear. She was brassy, Moira decided. She probably practised being theatrical in the mirror.

"Well, I certainly don't want to have another affair," Moira said. "And I don't know about you, but I could have done without the one I had."

She reached into her purse for a cigarette, her first since noon. Although Mrs. Hanna hadn't asked her not to smoke in the shop, she didn't want to be responsible for the smoky residue settling on everything.

"You have too many regrets, Moira," Carly said, digging in her purse for her own cigarettes. "For example, how many times have I heard you say you wish you could quit smoking?"

"Doesn't everybody want to quit?" Moira asked, watching the smoke drift from between her fingers. "Don't you?"

"No," Carly said. "No, I don't. I like smoking. Anyway, they say the damage is reversible. I'll quit when I start to cough blood."

"You don't mean that," Moira said.

"I do. And you should be more like me. You'd have more fun."

"I suppose I would," Moira said as the waiter approached with their drinks. "But then I'd have even more regrets."

Carly had ordered a *Beachport Bongo* and Moira had done the same to avoid having to choose from the hundred and one exotic concoctions on the drink menu. The waiter set the drinks on the table and Moira stared at the heavy plastic glasses shaped like upside-down bongo drums. Carly burst into laughter and the waiter looked perturbed.

"You want to pay now or run a tab?" he asked.

"It's the glasses," Moira said to him as she paid for the drinks. "She thinks the glasses are funny."

"Is that all," the waiter mumbled as he left. "I thought maybe I had spinach on my teeth."

Carly laughed harder, so hard Moira became embarrassed.

"Oh God," Carly said, dabbing at the corners of her eyes with the sleeve of her cotton shirt. "I love this place. It really kills me."

After she'd managed to stop laughing, Carly got up and headed for the washroom. Moira watched her stride confidently across the room, her purse slung over her shoulder, and thought for a moment maybe she should be more like Carly. Women like Carly seemed to bounce back so quickly. Whether the recovery was superficial or not was beside the point. They took chances, made themselves visible, and before you knew it they had another man. Carly seemed to have had several while Moira was away in Vancouver. Moira had consciously tried not to appear too interested in the details.

While she was waiting for Carly to come back, Moira looked around her. Not far from their table was a large aquarium on a stand. Moira's eyes drifted through the plastic plants and she tried to determine what kind of fish were hiding in the under-water jungle. One large fish, a Siamese Fighting Fish perhaps, hovered at the back of the tank. It was partially obscured by plants and by bursts of tiny bubbles pulsing out and upward from an air stone sitting on a bed of pink gravel. The sound of the pump was comforting. Moira sipped her drink and tried not to think of the number of calories. She wished she'd ordered a light beer instead.

Seated at a nearby table were a man and a woman, both grey-haired. They reminded Moira of the clay couple in *The Market Garden*, only instead of vegetables, they had packages from Eaton's and The Bay piled neatly against the legs of their chairs. Moira watched as the waiter placed a luscious fruit salad in the middle of their table. A hollowed-out pineapple overflowed with pale yellow chunks of fruit, and the top was dotted with maraschino cherries. The two ate from the same dish without speaking. Moira pretended she was the woman, tried to picture herself thirty-five years older. Would she reach across the table and run her fingers through the old man's hair?

When Carly returned, Moira didn't share the old couple with her. She was afraid Carly would think they were part of the decor.

"Well," said Carly, after she'd sat down and had a sip of her drink. "Are you going to tell me about him or not?"

Moira didn't want to, but couldn't think of a way to get out of it.

"Come on," Carly prodded. "What's the big secret? He was married. So let's have the rest of it."

"I just want to forget it," Moira said. "I don't want to keep reminding myself of a stupid mistake."

"What's wrong with a mistake or two?" Carly asked. "You've heard of the spice of life?"

"Oh for God's sake, Carly," Moira blurted out. "You can't wait to share every intimate detail of your life. Well, I'm not like that. There are a few things I want to keep to myself."

Carly looked hurt. Moira turned away and nervously tapped her empty bongo drum up and down on the table. The silence was awkward, but Moira was glad she'd finally said what was on her mind.

After what seemed like ages, Carly spoke. "I don't believe I've told you I had an abortion when I was with Bill," she said coldly. "Is that an intimate enough detail for you? I did manage to keep it to myself, you'll note."

Moira was genuinely shocked, not so much that Carly had had an abortion, but that she hadn't told everybody. Moira didn't know how to respond, whether or not to say she was sorry. Before she could say anything, Carly began to giggle.

"Oh God, Moira," she said. "You're right about me. I've got the biggest mouth in the world. I don't know how I managed to keep that a secret." She stopped giggling and tossed her hair back defiantly. "Bill told me not to tell anyone," she went on.

"But who the hell cares? I don't owe him anything. I'm glad it's out. Now it's just a story."

Just a story, Moira thought. So that's it. It had nothing to do with morality or guilt after all. Moira pried then, helped Carly to make it just a story.

"Did you want to have the baby?" she asked.

"Not really," Carly said. "When I first found out I was pregnant I hoped Bill would leave his wife. I soon figured out there wasn't a chance, baby or no baby. So I let him take me to New York for three days. The day after I had the abortion we went to a Broadway play and then had supper at this fabulous restaurant. He paid for it all, of course. And you know the rest. After we got back I broke it off. There are lots of fish in the sea, I figured. I didn't need him."

And you know the rest, Moira had heard Carly say. But she didn't know the rest. There was one whole chunk of the story missing.

"What about his wife?" she asked Carly.

"His wife?" Carly looked at Moira, puzzled. "I don't know anything about his wife," she said. "I suppose they're still together. I don't really care."

The old couple caught Moira's attention again as they stood and gathered up their shopping bags. Moira watched them make their way slowly to the door, then she began to speak.

"I met him in the bookstore where I worked," she said. "His name was Steve. He used to come in and look through the travel books." She lit another cigarette, then set it down in the ashtray.

"You don't have to tell me, Moira," Carly said. "Don't tell me if you don't want to."

"No, I want to," Moira said. Maybe it would work for her the way it worked for Carly.

"For a long time I didn't know he was married, and when I found out, he convinced me it didn't matter. Then we started going to their place while she was at work. She was a nurse. One night when Steve was in the shower I went through her drawers. She kept a bar of perfumed soap in with her underwear."

Carly looked uncomfortable, but Moira didn't care. Now that she'd started, she couldn't stop.

"There was a nightgown in one of the drawers, white cotton with a little embroidery. Nothing special, just a nightgown. I took it to the mirror and held it up to myself. I wanted to see her, but I couldn't. Even when I squinted my eyes, it was still me. So I took off my clothes and put it on. And when Steve got out of the shower, there I was."

Moira stopped speaking. She was somewhere else, smelling of scented toilet soap. She heard Carly's voice.

"What did he do?"

"Nothing," Moira said as the perfume faded. "He didn't do anything. I got dressed and left. The next day I quit my job."

There, Moira thought. It was just a story, like Carly's abortion.

The waiter came by and asked them if they wanted another round of drinks. They both said no, and he picked up their glasses and the empty pineapple skin from the old couple's table. As he was leaving, Moira called out to him.

"What kind of fish is that?" she asked, pointing to the aquarium.

The waiter looked at the tank, then back at Moira.

"Plastic," he said. "Some kind of plastic fish."

Moira stared at him. "Why in the world have you got an air stone in there? You don't need an air stone for plastic fish."

"Tell the manager lady," the waiter said, as though Moira and Carly had been nothing but trouble.

"Oh God," Carly said, as they put their coats on. "This place is really nuts."

Outside, little balls of sleet were blowing down the pavement. Moira wasn't surprised, it often snowed in October. She watched Carly run to catch her bus, then quickly crossed the street to the mailbox. It was dark, but Moira could easily see by the light of the street lamp. Shivering, wishing she had her fur-lined gloves along, she took the postcard from her pocket.

As she was about to drop it in the mail slot, she was tempted to read what the man had written to his wife. She hesitated, then held the card up to the light. At first she was puzzled by what she read.

Miss you Lil. Lunch next Tuesday?

There was no signature, no last name before the Vancouver address. Moira read it again, then began to laugh.

"Just a story, right?" she called out, and the wind carried her voice into the night. She opened her hand and let the wind take the clay couple on the postcard too. So much for that, Moira thought, remembering the carefully wrapped goblet. She could almost hear it crack.

THE CLEARING

"Two things I remember about Andy Penn," my mother said to me the day of his funeral. "The way he used to pour his coffee into his saucer and the time he came out of the bush with blood on his shirt." She paused before the bit about the blood, looking at me as if, after all these years, I might have something to tell her.

"And his glass eye," I said quickly. "I remember his glass eye."

It was three or four days after Christmas, more than twenty years after Andy Penn worked for us. We were sitting at the kitchen table looking out over the snowy field between the house and the bush. I loved to sit at the table as a child, eating breakfast, watching to see if anything would wander out from between the trees to paw at the stubble. Most mornings there were jumpers, sometimes an elk, sometimes a moose. The coyotes had a path through the field and although we hardly ever saw them, you could always find their tracks. When you were out walking, you could feel them watching you.

"A glass eye," said my mother. "Yes, I guess I do remember that. Although I wouldn't have if you hadn't mentioned it."

"He cleaned it in the washhouse," I said. "I used to hide outside and try to get a look at it. I wanted to see it when it wasn't in his eye."

"Good Lord," she said. "Did he take it right out?"

I nodded and took a sip of coffee.

"How did you know that?" she asked.

"I just knew," I said. "That's why the washcloths were so black."

"Oh, you just thought that up," said my mother. "How could he take it right out? And how could it get that dirty? You must

65

have been mistaken. You know how kids are, always coming up with one thing or another. You never know what they're thinking."

I considered that. Was it possible the glass eye was permanent and the dirt on the washcloth was plain old dirt from Andy Penn's face?

"And you were the worst little girl for coming up with things there ever was," my mother went on. "In your own world three quarters of the time. Honestly, it's a wonder you turned out normal."

He told me not to tell and I never did. They asked me about it, about the blood on his shirt, and I said as little as possible. He went into the bush, I said, and when he came out he had blood on his shirt.

That much I thought I could say. Andy had come running out of the bush and leapt into the truck, clutching his shoulder, blood oozing out from between the fingers of his hand. He got blood on the steering wheel and when he brushed the hair out of his eyes he got some on his forehead. I was terrified. What if he died on the way home? There was the tent, I thought, we could stop there for help, but as we rounded the bend and it came into view, I saw the woman. I saw the knife in her hand and I saw the blood on it. I had never been afraid of her before, had never been able to figure out why Old Arneson from down the road was always ranting and raving about her. Now I was afraid. And there was Andy Penn bleeding to death beside me in the truck.

But he didn't die, didn't even come close.

"Don't worry," Andy said to me as we came out of the bush and turned onto the grid road. "It's nothing much."

He sounded calm enough. My heart stopped pounding. When we got home, instead of parking by the house, Andy dropped me off at the approach.

"You won't say anything, will you?" Andy said to me.

I shook my head.

My dad, recovering from his operation, was walking around the yard, stretching his legs. He got a look at Andy as I climbed out of the truck.

"Where's Andy going?" my dad asked me.

"I don't know," I said.

We walked to the house and I could tell he was not quite satisfied.

"That was blood on Andy's shirt, wasn't it?" he asked.

"Yeah," I said, not looking at him.

"What happened?"

"I don't know," I said. "I was in the truck. He went into the bush and when he came out he had blood on his shirt."

They asked me more questions, but I didn't tell them anything else. When Andy came home he had a bandage wrapped around his shoulder and a new shirt on. It still had the wrinkles in it from the package. My dad asked him where he found a new shirt on a Sunday, and Andy said Fisher's garage, it was always open. He said he fell on his axe, lucky thing he didn't chop his own head off. And that was all. They didn't push him too much because they were used to him.

"Well, did you find any blueberries before Andy almost chopped his head off?" my mother asked me later.

"No," I said. "I guess she got them all again." I made myself say that. I didn't want to talk about her, but I thought it might look suspicious if I didn't say something about her.

"There weren't many people at the funeral," my mother said. "I'm glad we heard about it. Luck, that's all it was. We never would have heard if your father hadn't had to go clear over to Fox River for parts."

"Well, I'm glad we went," I said.

"It was nice to see a few of his people there," my mother said. "I didn't think he had any, to tell you the truth. Of course, he talked so little you never knew what was in his head."

"He was shy," I said.

"Was he? I never saw it that way. I thought he was — you know — an oddball. I suppose that's why he never married."

"He was just shy," I said, pushing my chair back from the table, thankful that my parents had a new bathroom and I wasn't going to have to go outside. "He didn't know how to talk to people."

She sat, then, turning her coffee cup round and round on the table, puzzling over Andy Penn twenty years after the fact.

"Maybe we shouldn't have let you ride around with him in that truck," she said. "Nowadays people would talk. I just didn't think about it at the time. Lord, I would hate to find out people talked. Wouldn't you?"

I just laughed and closed the bathroom door.

Inside the medicine cabinet, the old jar was still sitting on a shelf, my name on the prescription label. It occurred to me, as it did every time I opened the cabinet, that the jar should be thrown out. But I knew why it was there. My mother thought I might need it again. She was afraid that some night, home on a visit, I might wake up scratching my skin raw. She needed to know the old cream was there to relieve the terrible itching and heal the wounds.

The itching caused me to miss a lot of school. If I'd had a particularly bad night I got to stay home the next day. Once, I stayed home for a whole year. I had missed so much school my parents decided it would be better to wait until the next September to send me back. "Just for the rest of this year," they told me, apologizing. "It will take the pressure off you to catch up." But I didn't need apologies or explanations. I was twelve years old. I hated the red spots. On the school bus one of the boys said I had leprosy and nobody would sit with me. I wanted to stay home forever.

Andy Penn was at our place that year and I was like his shadow, hanging around the barn, riding with him in his truck, sometimes going to auction sales where we stood away from the crowd and never bid on anything. I tried once. I moved up to the front to bid on a transistor radio the auctioneer was holding up. But I wasn't fast enough and I accidentally bought an old bedspring and Andy had to load it into the back of the truck and drive it to the dump before we went home. I didn't have to ask him not to tell. At the auction sale he just went along and pretended we bought the bedspring on purpose and when we got home neither of us said anything about it. That night I woke up with my skin on fire. I scratched my arms and legs until they bled and my mother had to get up and heat water so I could have a bath. She poured some kind of crystals into the water, something the doctor gave her to stop the itching. Then she lathered me all over with the cool, soothing cream. It made the bedsheets stick to me, but I didn't care because it put out the fire.

I didn't need the cream anymore. I looked at it in the medicine cabinet and considered throwing it out myself. My mother's need to keep it, though, seemed private so I left it on the shelf and closed the cabinet door.

THE CLEARING

When I came out of the bathroom my father was sitting at the kitchen table stirring sugar into his coffee. He'd apparently finished whatever it was he'd been doing outside.

"A damn good worker," he was saying. "Andy Penn was the best worker we ever had on the place."

"Those were the days," my mother said as I sat down and poured myself another cup. "A good man would work for room and board and a few extra dollars. Nowadays we can hardly look at hiring a man for the summer, what with high wages and the price of wheat."

"Don't need a hired man," my dad said, reaching under the table to pinch her. "I can always hook you up to the plough, if worse comes to worst."

My mother shrieked and I felt myself blushing as I always do when my dad teases her. This teasing was such a mystery to me, like so many things that happened between them. There seemed to be so much that others shouldn't see. I used to imagine my mother taking her clothes off in front of my dad. I wondered if she was embarrassed. I would be, I decided.

Once I asked my mother if she thought Andy had a girlfriend. He used to go into town on Saturday nights and come home late. I was relieved by her answer.

"I'd be surprised," she said. "Some people just aren't cut out for marrying. Andy's one of them, I suppose. It's hard to imagine him being — intimate with anyone."

I knew what that meant. I could understand why some weren't cut out for it. I decided there were people who could live perfectly well without taking their clothes off for anybody. Andy seemed happy enough. He was lucky, I thought. Who wanted to take their clothes off anyway? Even if you didn't have red splotches, who would want to? I was never going to take my clothes off in front of a man.

I smiled to myself now, thinking about that. It turned out it wasn't so bad, not even the first time.

My dad finished his coffee and said, "What the hell, might as well have another cup." He said he supposed the place wouldn't fall apart if he quit work early on the day of Andy Penn's funeral. I poured it for him and sat down again by the kitchen window. I looked out across the field at the line of bush. I could still imagine that tent, the white one, in a clearing three or four miles in.

I saw Andy speak to her only once. It was on the way into the bush the day he bled all over the truck. He stopped on the trail in front of her tent, told me to wait, and walked over to where she was standing with a half dozen or so dead rabbits on the grass in front of her. When he came back, I waited for him to say something, like "she told me the berries are good this year" or "there's a spot just north of that stand of black poplar." I waited for him to tell me what they were laughing about. But he didn't.

"Why do you let her go through?" Old Arneson asked my dad more than once. "You could put up a gate with a sign on it. No trespassing, you could say. She'd have to find another way in then, set up her goddamned teepee in somebody else's part of the bush."

"She doesn't hurt anything," my dad said.

"She gets to the blueberries first. Just ask your missus if she don't."

She did get the blueberries first. That was the reason she was there, that and the Seneca root. She'd come in the summer with her wagonload of kids to dig Seneca. Afterward, the forest floor would be speckled with little holes. She sold gunny sacks full of roots to the drug companies (for good money, Old Arneson said) and then, about the end of August, the blueberries would be ready.

My mother didn't care about the blueberries. We always made one trip into the bush on a Sunday. "Let's just check," she would say and we'd pack the lunch box and head out in the truck. We'd pass the tent and sometimes they were there but we never waved or honked or shouted hello. We stared at them and they stared at us and that's just the way it was. And we never found any blueberries, but we'd stop in a little clearing that was surrounded by seventy-foot poplars waving in the breeze like flagpoles.

It was so quiet in there. You could hear the leaves, the odd squirrel or maybe a crow. But mostly, you noticed the silence. We never talked much while we ate our lunch in the clearing and sometimes, if it was sunny, my dad would lie back and take a nap. It's the only place I've ever seen him have a nap outside.

"Roll up your pant legs," my mother would say to me. "Let the sun shine on that skin. Sun's an antiseptic, you know." So I would roll up my pant legs and my sleeves and let the sun shine on me. After a while we'd get back in the truck and drive out of the bush. That would be that for another year. The next day my mother and I would take the pails a hundred yards behind the house and find all the blueberries we needed.

The summer Andy's shoulder got cut, I overheard Old Arneson giving Andy advice. They were sawing old logs into stove lengths and had stopped for a smoke break. I was hanging around, as usual, but Old Arneson wasn't paying any attention to me. "You won't get anywhere with women in town," he told Andy. "Not with that eyeball, you won't. But that squaw in the bush, she's there for the taking."

My face burned, but I couldn't leave because then they would know I'd heard and that would be worse. I watched Andy pull tobacco from his leather pouch, lay it carefully on the paper and roll it up with his yellow fingers. I waited while he struck a match on his jeans and lit the cigarette. I prayed he wouldn't say anything. He smoked his cigarette and then he pulled on the cord to start the saw up again. Old Arneson shook his head and walked over to the bush. I could tell he was unzipping his fly. When he was done he turned around and saw me watching him. He winked.

My dad waved his hand in front of my face.
"What are you staring at out there?" he said.
"Just thinking about Old Arneson," I said.
"Crazy old coot," said my mother. "Sits in his kitchen and watches TV all day."
"He makes out all right," said my dad.
"He lives in filth." My mother was more disgusted by filth than by anything else. "Someone should call the Health people. He should be moved out of that place and a match set to it."
"He bought a dish," my dad told me. "Gets over fifty channels, I hear."
"He still swears like a trooper." My mother looked at me. "He always did have the foulest mouth. We shouldn't have let you anywhere near him. Who knows what you picked up listening to him."

"I didn't hang around him much," I said. "I didn't like the way he talked to Andy, like he was better than him."

"Don't be too hard on him," my dad said. "A lot of people thought they were better than Arneson. Just the way things are around here."

The August after I missed a year of school my dad's appendix burst. My mother waited on him hand and foot for two weeks while he recuperated. She didn't want to leave him to go into the bush looking for blueberries, so she packed a picnic lunch and sent Andy Penn and me as though it was a necessary ritual.

"Just go and have a look," she said. "In case they've missed a good patch."

"Maybe check a stand of trees for firewood while you're in there," my dad said to Andy, giving him a real reason for going. He needn't have though. Andy accepted the trip into the bush to look for berries like it was part of the job.

The trip was fine with me. I liked riding around with Andy. He had two big plastic dice hanging from the windshield and a pine-scented air freshener under the dash. Sometimes I dared to pretend I was Andy's girl friend. It was safe with him.

Because it was Sunday, Andy had a clean shirt on. And he wore a cowboy hat instead of his usual John Deere cap. I closed my eyes and pretended we were going steady.

As we approached the tent on the way in, Andy slowed down, then stopped. I was surprised.

"You wait here," he said to me. He walked over to the woman, who was standing with the dead rabbits on the ground in front of her. Her kids stopped running around to stare at Andy. I saw him speak to her, then she pointed north along the trail. Andy said something else and they both laughed. I suddenly felt as if I was watching my parents, watching my father pinch my mother's bottom, watching my mother unbutton her blouse, knowing my father was in the room with her. I remembered what Old Arneson had said.

When Andy got back to the truck I waited for him to tell me what they were laughing about, but of course he didn't. We drove north to where the tall poplars were and poked around looking for blueberries in the clearing. We found the plants, but there wasn't a berry on them.

"Not enough rain, maybe," I said, hoping Andy would say something. "She told me she beat us to it," I thought he might say. Or, "She said we can go ahead and look, but we won't find any kind of berry for miles around here." That would be enough to make Andy laugh, I thought, if she'd said it in a friendly kind of way. But Andy wasn't about to tell me anything.

We ate our lunch in the clearing, bologna sandwiches with lots of mustard, and butter tarts for dessert. It was an unusually hot day in the bush. There weren't even any mosquitoes.

Andy lay down on the grass to have a nap, just like my dad, shielding his eyes from the sun with his cowboy hat. You couldn't tell there was anything wrong with him at all. I decided to roll up my pant legs and let the sun shine on my bare skin. I managed to get my jeans up over my knees with a little tugging, then I lay back and looked up at the tops of the poplars. The sun felt wonderful and I imagined what it would be like to lie on a beach on a desert island somewhere. If you were all alone, you could lie there naked. I squinted my eyes and pretended the poplars were palm trees. Some of the leaves were already starting to yellow, and I turned them into bunches of bananas. What would it be like to live in a tropical country, I wondered. Some place where nobody wore clothes, no matter what they looked like. A magpie swooped through the open space between the tree tops above me and I closed my eyes to pretend it was a cockatoo or a parrot with blue and orange feathers.

I opened my eyes. Andy was sitting up, staring at my bare legs, and his big calloused hand was hovering over one of the ugly red spots. He didn't see that my eyes were open. I lay there, my heart pounding, and thought that his hand above my leg was like me hiding outside the washhouse trying to get a look at his eye. He lowered his hand to touch the spot. I held my breath. He moved his hand up to my knee.

I jumped, frantically tugging at my pant legs.

"They're just about gone," I stammered. My jeans were stuck over one knee and I pushed and twisted to get them down. "The doctor says there'll be scars, but if I don't ever wear shorts maybe nobody will notice."

Andy stood up, slapped the grass off his pants, and put his hat back on his head. He picked up the lunch box and put it in the truck. When I finally got my pant legs down, we started home.

We hadn't passed the tent yet, but we were close to it when Andy stopped.

"I'm going into the bush for a minute," he said. "Gotta check that stand of trees for your dad."

He took his axe from the back of the truck and he went into the bush.

I turned the key to listen to the radio, even though the reception was bad in the bush. I pulled my pant legs down to cover the space between the tops of my socks and my jeans. I stuffed my hands in my pockets so I wouldn't have to look at the spots.

It wasn't long before Andy was back, blood oozing from his shoulder. He jumped into the truck, started it up fast, and drove out of the bush. When we passed the tent, the woman was standing there with the knife in her hand. And I saw blood on it.

"You won't say anything, will you?" Andy said to me as I got out of the truck. I shook my head.

That was something, ending up at Andy Penn's funeral. I stayed home until New Year's and then my dad drove me to Saskatoon to catch my flight back to Winnipeg.

"Don't know why you have to live so far away from home," he said as we were waiting for my flight to be called.

"Now Dad, don't start that," I said. "If you'd try flying you could come and visit me more often. You could come for a weekend whenever you felt like it."

"Well anyway," he said, "good thing Andy Penn died when he did. I figure he'd have been glad you were there."

My flight was called and I boarded with my Christmas presents and settled into my seat. I thought about Andy. I suppose he would have been glad I was there. I found myself looking at my hands, looking at the red spots, so faint now they didn't seem worth worrying about.

REAL FAMOUS MEN

Sari had been hearing about Marty Beuler's parties for over a year, ever since she started work at the library. Marty would entertain at coffee on Monday mornings by telling anecdotes about people none of them knew: Nita Sellers ("her toga fell off on the dot of midnight and she just kept right on dancing, stark naked"); Gloria Stadnick and her husband Bob ("they came with *other* people, if you know what I mean"); Grant McInnis ("he finally came out of the closet — my God, everyone's known for years he was gay"); Colby Pratt ("he brought his mountain climbing gear and scaled the outside wall — made a fantastic entrance through the patio doors"). Marty told the stories so well that Sari came to think of these people as famous, as though she had read about them in one of her magazines.

Sari did not for a minute dream that she would ever be witness to one of Marty's parties, so it took her completely by surprise when he stopped at her desk one Thursday afternoon and extended an invitation.

"It will be madness," he assured her. "Absolute madness." He leaned closer. "This gorgeous eligible male named Buzz will be stopping by," he whispered. "All the single gals I know pop their corks for him."

This embarrassed Sari and she quickly tried to think of something to say to cover up. Marty would expect an amusing response.

"He sounds like an astronaut," she said.

Marty laughed.

"See you about eight," he said, then slapped his hand over his mouth and looked around secretively. Sari could imagine him chanting "no more joiners".

75

THE WEDNESDAY FLOWER MAN

For the rest of the afternoon Sari sat at her desk and tried to figure out why she had been invited. It seemed the rest of the staff, all of whom had been there much longer than her, were destined only to hear about the parties. She decided it must be her age. She, at twenty-seven, was the only one under thirty. Marty himself must be at least thirty, but Sari supposed he was one of those men who didn't plan to marry until they had gotten youth well out of their systems. He had had six girl friends that she knew of in the past year. He would come in to work every two months and say, "Well, I've broken another heart. She wanted to get serious, if you know what I mean." People would laugh, especially Mrs. Bedford. Her hair was as white as snow and she looked to be at least sixty, but she flirted with Marty as though they were high school sweethearts. Mrs. Bedford would actually be jealous, Sari thought, if she knew Sari had been invited to one of his famous parties. Sari thought Marty was all right, but he was too affected, definitely not her type.

She was torn about whether or not she should actually go to the party. On one hand, she had fantasies going back a long way about attending parties just like this one. There would probably be drugs and designer clothes. And men, competent men, who really knew what they were doing. Men like Colby Pratt and this Buzz guy Marty mentioned.

But on the other hand, such a party was bound to turn her into a nervous wreck. She had to admit she didn't have a great track record with that kind of man. Famous men, she called them. Men who stood out in a crowd. She was drawn to them the way some women seem to be drawn to the intellectual type. Intellect didn't matter to Sari, just that strong presence of a man who knows he can have whatever woman he chooses.

Sari wondered if she could really handle one of them, if she could pull it off. Actually having contact was a little different from sitting comfortably in her living room with her notebook of anecdotes and her glossy magazine photographs. Would she know what to say to a real famous man? She might not. She could always act mysterious. Men were attracted to mysterious women. But what if she blew it and came out looking like a fool? Marty might end up telling stories about her. She wouldn't mind that, as long as she looked somewhat victorious or even interesting, but she wouldn't want to look stupid, or worse, as if she couldn't handle herself around a certain type of man.

In the end, the decision was fairly easy to make. She had to go to Marty's party. She couldn't pass up an opportunity, not when she had mingled so often in her own mind with the likes of Buzz and Colby. If she really blew it, she could always quit work and find a new job, start life over where nobody knew anything about her.

Inadvertently, she arrived early. It didn't take as long as she thought it would to get to Marty's apartment building, and it was winter, too cold to wait outside in her car for half an hour. She decided she could tell Marty she'd come to help him get ready, lay out the hors d'oeuvres or rinse wine glasses. That was appropriate, she thought, for someone he worked with.

She pushed the security buzzer.

"Garden of earthly delights," Marty's sing-song voice said, distorted and distant through the speaker.

"It's Sari."

"Sari, Sari, quite contrary," his voice sang. Then the security door buzzed and Sari stepped inside. She rode the elevator to the tenth floor, where she found Marty's door wide open.

"Won't people complain?" she asked him as he took her coat and hung it in the closet. "I mean, don't you have to worry about noise and all that?"

"Not here," Marty said. "We call this Party Plaza. Anyone who doesn't like it has to move out. It's in the lease."

"Oh," Sari said and followed Marty to the kitchen. She noticed he was wearing the same grey flannel pants he'd worn to work that day, only he'd changed into a black and yellow checked shirt and a cowboy string tie. She herself had worn what she hoped was an alluring black dress. It occurred to her that she might have over-dressed. She could take off her jewellery if she had to, she thought. She had on her grandmother's chunky red glass necklace and earrings.

Marty poured some white wine into a plastic glass and handed it to her.

"What can I do?" Sari asked.

"About what?" Marty asked. "Just lay it on me. I love personal problems."

"To help," Sari said, rolling her eyes. "What can I do to help?"

"Oh," Marty said. "How disappointing. Here. Take this into the living room. Pass it around if you like."

He handed her a Tupperware bowl full of ripple potato chips. Sari looked at the bowl.

"I thought you'd have caviar," she quipped, pleased with herself.

"Well, aren't you the rude thing," Marty responded, placing his hands affectedly on his hips. "Your mother ought to have taught you some manners."

Sari tossed him a saucy look and carried the bowl into the living room where there was only one woman to pass it to. She was sitting on the couch leafing through what was apparently Marty's scrapbook. She turned down the chips.

"I'm a vegetarian," she said, briefly looking up at Sari. "They're cooked in animal fat."

Sari sat down and took a *People* magazine from the rack beside the couch. The other woman was wearing jeans and a T-shirt. Sari wondered about slipping her jewellery off, then decided to wait and see what other people were wearing. It was her understanding that vegetarianism was on the way out.

People magazine was not Sari's favourite. You could pick up a few interesting details but the photography was frustrating. This particular issue had some juicy bits in it about Sean Penn, but nothing you could really sink your teeth into. He was too young anyway. Young men always seemed like boys playing games to her, just one step removed from the high school locker room.

The other woman kept laughing out loud at things in the scrapbook. Sari wondered why in the world anyone would leave their scrapbook on a coffee table for people, strangers even, to look at? It made her curious about what was in it. Sari thought about her own notebooks and how embarrassing it would be if anyone else found out about them.

She flipped through the magazine, then placed it carefully back in the rack. As she did so, a gorgeous male face peered up at her from another glossy cover. It was Warren Beatty. She picked up the magazine and ran her fingers over his cheek bones. How had she missed this one? Warren Beatty didn't appear on a cover very often, he was so private. The article was on page seventeen. Sari turned to it and read about how easy it was for him to find women to go to bed with. One woman was quoted as saying he had once pulled her into the bathroom at a party and made love to her on the floor. They hadn't even been introduced.

Sari noted the date on the cover of the magazine, hoping she'd still be able to find it somewhere, then placed it back in the rack. She heard the buzzer. "Garden of earthly delights," she heard Marty sing into the intercom. Good. More people. Sari found it awkward sitting with a woman who didn't seem to want to talk. She looked around, waiting for whoever was on the way up in the elevator.

Marty's living room was nondescript. It was painted an interesting enough colour, dark rose, but other than that nothing stood out as interesting or different or reflective of Marty's personality. It's not that Sari was expecting a jacuzzi in the living room or anything like that, but a bizarre piece of sculpture or some unusual prints would not have been out of character. A cheaply framed reproduction of one of Tom Thompson's famous trees, hanging crookedly on one wall, was not what she'd expected. There was the scrapbook, which the other woman was still looking at. Sari would have to try to get hold of that later.

A number of voices (all female, it seemed) entered the apartment and Sari heard Marty oohing and awing over something someone was wearing. A woman in a bright purple dress came into the living room and sat next to Sari. The dress was definitely on the gaudy side, with several layers of swishy polyester, but it made Sari feel better about having dressed up.

"My name is Patricia," the woman said to Sari, ignoring the woman leafing through the scrapbook. "I haven't seen you here before."

"No," Sari said. "My first time."

Marty entered the room with several other women, one of them hanging on his arm. She wore a black leotard with a green garbage bag over top, cinched at the waist with a heavy studded belt. She was the only one Marty introduced to Sari and her name was Norma Jean. Sari wondered if she was Marty's latest.

"Now Patricia," Marty said to the woman in the purple dress. "I hope you're not going to let this little incident stop you from having a really good time tonight."

"What incident?" the woman reading the scrapbook said, looking up. "What now?" She apparently knew all these women.

"Patricia's sister's husband is after her again," Marty said. "Isn't he Patty?"

"He phoned me twice last week," Patricia said. "He says he wants to talk about Lucy's problems, but I know what's really going on. The son-of-a-bitch. I've got a mind to tell Lucy."

The buzzer went again and Marty whipped out to the hallway.

"I'm going down to put a brick in the door," he said.

Norma Jean flopped down next to Sari on the couch.

"I love your jewels," she said, reaching toward Sari and lifting her heavy necklace. "Where'd you get it?"

"Thank you," Sari responded, uncomfortable because all the women were now looking at her. "It was my grandmother's."

"I wish my grandmother would die," Norma Jean said, dropping the necklace. "She's got some great jewellery."

Sari found herself laughing, even though no one else was. She should perhaps have been offended, she'd been very close to her grandmother, but it was so much what she expected. She could hear Marty telling the story at work: "Norma Jean's actually waiting for her grandmother to die so she can grab her costume jewellery — can you believe it?"

Sari's grandmother had collected pictures of the royals with a fervour. Sari remembered going through her scrapbooks when she was a little girl, with her grandmother pointing out Lady So-and-so and what she wore to such-and-such royal wedding. She'd encouraged Sari when she was very young to start collecting pictures of movie and television stars. At first, before she found out about movie star magazines, Sari dutifully cut pictures out of the newspaper or *Maclean's* magazine, which her father read. But at twelve years old she discovered the real thing, *Movie World* and *Teen Idol*, and her collection started in earnest. About that time, she gave up on pictures of women and limited her collection to men, heading off on her own from her grandmother's interest in the famous. She began writing letters to fan clubs and to addresses she gleaned from the TV guides, asking for autographed photos.

She began to think about these famous men every waking minute of her day, figured out the time difference between her and Hollywood or New York, tried to guess what they might be doing while she was having lunch, while she was having a bath, while she was lying in bed at night before she went to sleep. She lost touch with the other kids at school, was contented to come home every day and work on her pictures.

By the time she reached high school, the pictures weren't enough. She started to dream at night about contact, about Paul

McCartney touching her hair, about Clint Eastwood wrapping his strong arms around her, about Robert Redford kissing her on the mouth. She began looking around at school for suitable substitutes. None of the boys in her own grade would do, of course, but some of the older ones, the star basketball players, the rich ones with expensive clothes and their own cars — somehow they seemed like possibilities. Except that they weren't the least bit interested in her and she had no idea, absolutely none, how you went about attracting their attention. So the famous men in her school ended up the same place as the other famous men in her life, on her bulletin board or in her scrapbook. She cut pictures out of the school newspaper and dreamed she was dancing with the star quarterback of the football team.

When Sari was in grade ten, her school had a Sadie Hawkins dance. That meant the girls got to phone up the boys and invite them to be their dates. It was too good to be true. Sari lay awake for weeks beforehand trying to choose which boy to invite. She finally settled on one. His name was Leroy. He was the provincial javelin champion and he turned her down. So did Brian and Ross and Murray. Sari told herself she'd waited too long and they were already taken. Really, though, what she'd learned was that even on Sadie Hawkins Day you had to wait to be chosen. Especially when you were dealing with famous men.

Sari sat in Marty's bathroom and looked at the floor. She had a hard time imagining two people making out on it, but she supposed the bathroom that hosted Warren Beatty and whoever it was had been much more elegant.

She'd had several glasses of wine and was tired of waiting for the more interesting people to show up. She considered going home. Who was she kidding, anyway, that Colby or Buzz or any other male would waste a minute of his time on her? She should know he wouldn't from past experience. She'd had one little fling in university with a mildly famous guy named Bogie (that's what his friends called him) and it had been nerve-wracking and, finally, disappointing. He'd chosen her from across the room in the cafeteria. She supposed it was because she had just had her hair dyed red and it really was rather attractive. The first time they went out on a date Sari got so excited she threw up before he picked her up. They went to a 3-D soft porn movie and Sari couldn't get the glasses to work. She figured out toward the end that she'd been wearing them upside-down. They went to his place afterward. Sari decided on the way there that she would sleep with him; she had to, she thought, if she was to be taken seriously by a man who had his choice of women. He knew she was a virgin, she couldn't hide it, and he took it upon himself to introduce her to the fabulous world of sex. "I can't get enough of it," he told her. He did seem to get enough of it with her, though, and after a month or so he stopped calling. Sari was depressed for a while, but she attacked her collection with renewed vigour and soon felt better. Thinking about this, she decided to stay at the party a while longer. She had been chosen once. Maybe it was time to be chosen again.

She looked inside Marty's medicine cabinet and wondered how someone like Warren Beatty got away with it. What made women go with him so willingly? Maybe it was partly that aggressiveness that made him so attractive. Maybe, she thought, if you acted as though you could have anything you wanted, you really could have it. Maybe she'd been going about this wrong, waiting. Or even asking. On Sadie Hawkins Day she'd asked. Maybe you don't ask. Maybe you just take.

It was unfortunate, Sari thought, that Marty didn't keep condoms in his medicine cabinet. She should be prepared to assume that responsibility. She decided not to worry about it. She had a good look at the bathroom floor; it didn't look any too clean but she decided not to worry about that either, Warren Beatty wouldn't have. Then someone pounded on the door so she went to the kitchen for another glass of wine.

The music was loud. There must have been thirty people dancing in the living room. Marty had moved the couch and coffee table into a corner to make more room. Sari remembered the scrapbook and thought maybe now would be a good time to look through it, but she couldn't see it anywhere. She felt kind of silly standing there in the doorway, afraid that people would think no one had asked her to dance, even though it was true. They all seemed to know each other. She studied the people and tried to figure out if she knew any of them from Marty's stories. If she did, it wasn't obvious. There was no one there who looked like a Buzz or a Colby. That made sense, though. Their type would most likely arrive late.

When Sari actually studied the people dancing, they looked

surprisingly young. They must be university students, she thought, and wondered how Marty would know so many of them and what the attraction was. The woman in the purple dress, Patricia, seemed to be among the few exceptions. She looked to be about Marty's age. She was sitting on a footstool, staring straight ahead. Sari watched as she slowly toppled over sideways onto the floor. A few people dancing near her looked and laughed; other than that, she was pretty well ignored. Sari wondered if she was in the habit of passing out at parties. Maybe she'd worn the garish purple dress so no one would step on her.

A group of people sitting on the floor in a corner were smoking what Sari assumed was marijuana. Well, that was something, she thought. Not that she wanted any, but it at least fit with what she'd expected, even hoped for.

She saw a man, like Patricia, a little older than most of the others, coming toward her from across the room. Before she read the look on his face, it was too late.

"I've seen you trying to catch my eye," he shouted over the music, putting his arm around her shoulder.

"Oh, I don't think so," Sari shouted back. "I was just, you know, watching." She tried to slide out from under his arm but it moved with her.

"Don't be embarrassed," he said in her ear. "I think it's great when women make the first move. What's your name?"

"Sari," she said.

"Mine's Bob. Bob Stadnick."

"Gloria's husband?"

He quickly pulled his arm away. There was a lull in the music as someone changed the tape.

"What do you know about Gloria?" he snapped.

"Nothing," she said carefully, looking around to see if anyone was watching them. "I've just heard Marty talk about you two."

"Bitch," he said to her and walked away.

Sari's heart pounded and she was sure her cheeks were red. Who was he calling a bitch? Not her, surely. But it was her, she knew. Marty appeared at her side from somewhere.

"I should have warned you about Bob," he said, dragging her into the kitchen. "He's an absolute letch."

"Don't worry about it," Sari said, nonchalantly pouring herself another glass of wine. Who was she kidding? She didn't belong at this or any other party where people came on to you and called you bitch in two minutes flat. She would wait a while longer, then leave when no one was watching.

"Listen," Marty said, "Buzz will be here any minute. One look at him and the wait will be worth it."

"Just to see him?" Sari said, emptying her wine glass, trying to keep her hands from shaking. "I can see good-looking men on magazine covers whenever I want to."

Marty filled her glass again. "I just knew you'd be a wild one inside that quiet exterior," he said. "Quiet people are always aggressive when you get to know them."

Sari listened. A wild one? Aggressive? Yes, that's what she'd like to think about herself. That was the image, wasn't it, that got you what you wanted. She perked up. Maybe there was hope. She spun around drunkenly and went looking for Bob Stadnick.

"I wouldn't make eyes at you if somebody paid me," she said when she found him, then quickly headed for the bathroom and locked herself in. There. That was telling him, she thought. She looked in the mirror above the sink and after her eyes focussed she liked what she saw. Her cheeks were a little red, but that made her look healthy. Her hair was a bit dishevelled, but that was definitely sexy. She practiced a few different facial expressions and settled on a kind of moody, sensitive look.

Someone pounded on the door.

"Let me in. Quick," a woman's voice said.

Sari opened the door. It was Patricia. Her makeup was smudged around her eyes and one shoe was missing.

"Sorry," she said, stumbling into the bathroom. "But I can't wait."

Sari left and closed the door behind her. She was faced with the dancers again and they looked even younger than before. Norma Jean had taken off the garbage bag and was dancing in the black leotard, not with Marty. She had the studded belt slung over her shoulder.

Sari went to the kitchen and poured herself another drink. She leaned against the counter, looking at all the empty beer bottles piling up in the corner. Suddenly Marty appeared and grabbed her by the arm, leading her to the living room.

"Buzz is here," he said. "You absolutely have to meet him."

There was no mistaking him. He was indeed good-looking,

84

commanding the attention of everyone in the room by standing on top of Marty's coffee table, shaking up a bottle of champagne. Even above the music you could hear the loud pop.

"My God," Sari shouted in Marty's ear. "He even pops his own cork."

"Come on," Marty said. "I'll introduce you."

"Never mind," Sari said. "I'll introduce myself."

"You're a real tigress," Marty said. "I knew it. I just knew it."

Sari edged her way along the wall, past the Tom Thompson tree, toward the bathroom door. She picked a spot where she could keep her eye on Buzz, grab him when the time was right and duck into the bathroom. She couldn't believe she was actually going to do this, but what the hell, she told herself. If not now, then never. She caught Bob Stadnick glaring at her from across the room, had a brief loss of confidence thinking he might be the violent type, then assured herself someone, maybe even Buzz, would come to her rescue should he attack.

It wasn't hard keeping her eye on Buzz's whereabouts. He was tall and loud, and wherever he went a little swarm of women congregated around him. Sari waited, like a cat waiting to pounce on a mouse, watching people come and go from the bathroom, knowing when it was occupied and when it wasn't. She was pleased with herself. Her stomach wasn't the least bit upset. She had finally found a way to handle famous men.

Buzz was dancing with a blonde in a bright blue sweater and they were slowly moving toward Sari. When they were just a few feet away from her, she made one last check on the bathroom. Unoccupied. Then she stepped forward, grabbed his arm and pulled him inside, slamming the door behind her.

She was facing him, could see the back of his head in the mirror above the sink. She stared at him, not quite sure what to do now that she had him. His hair was dripping with champagne and he had a puzzled, uncertain expression on his face. He looked almost angry, she thought. Someone pounded on the bathroom door.

"Is this some kind of a joke?" Buzz said to her.

In the mirror Sari saw the plastic shower curtain move. She turned around and stared as Patricia, half asleep, emerged from behind the curtain like a bedraggled purple butterfly. She sat down on the toilet lid, pulling off her one high-heeled shoe.

"This has been a really shitty party," she said, as though there was nothing unusual about Buzz and Sari being in the bathroom together.

"Can I go now?" Buzz asked Sari with a decidedly nasty edge.

"I don't see why not," Sari said. "I don't know why you came in here in the first place. This is obviously the ladies' room."

He left and Sari stood awkwardly, trying to decide if it would be possible to leave the party with any dignity at all. Buzz was probably out there right now talking about what she'd done. If she left in a hurry, people might think she was embarrassed or humiliated. If she stayed, she would have to put up with being stared at for the rest of the night. When Patricia burst into tears, Sari quickly decided to have one dignified drink for the road, then go home.

Sari went straight to the kitchen without looking around and found Marty sitting at the table, tired, with a big bottle of Coke in front of him. It occurred to Sari that these parties were not nearly as much fun for him as he wanted people to think.

"Someone just complained about the noise," he said. "I can't believe it. They're letting absolute riff-raff move into this building."

"Is Norma Jean your current girl friend?" Sari asked, pouring herself a glass of wine.

"Norma Jean?" Marty looked old, maybe even forty. "Nah. She's a pain in the ass, Norma Jean is. I don't even invite her to these things. She just comes."

Sari downed the wine and stacked the plastic glass inside several others on the counter.

"I'm going home," she said.

"I'll see you out," Marty said, following her to the door. She found her coat under a heap of others on the floor. They walked to the elevator together and Sari pushed the button.

"Isn't Buzz something?" Marty said as they waited.

"Yeah," Sari answered. "Something. Too young for me though. Definitely immature."

She was conscious of Marty watching her pull on her mitts and tie her scarf. "I don't suppose you'd want to go to a movie with me sometime," he said.

"Maybe," she said.

In the elevator she thought about Marty's scrapbook, regretting that she hadn't found out what was inside. She felt left out. It was right there for all to see and had somehow escaped her.

On the way home, Sari stopped at an all-night drug store and picked up a few magazines, the one with Warren Beatty on the cover and the latest issue of *Rolling Stone*. She crawled into bed and tried to read about Bruce Willis, but her eyes wouldn't focus. She'd had too much to drink. She turned out the light, but she couldn't sleep either. She kept hearing Marty's voice: "Patricia Hayes actually passed out in my bathtub. Can you believe it?" Finally, Sari dropped off and dreamed about Mrs. Bedford's coy little laugh. All night long she heard Mrs. Bedford laughing, as though her high school sweetheart was teasing the pants off her.

GLORY DAYS

It was a four hour drive in heavy winter fog. The RCMP were advising people not to travel, but it was the day after Christmas so there were lots of cars on the road anyway. I drove with my lights on, hoping everyone else would do the same. It was my first trip back since my mother sold our house. She'd moved to the Okanagan the year after my father died, the year I went away to university.

I was apprehensive. I hadn't kept in touch with people the way Brad had. Once a year he would head out to the lake for a wild weekend with all his old home-town friends. I never wanted to go along, but at the same time was afraid to stay away. I suppose I was worried his friends would think he'd married a bitch. Of course, that's exactly what they think now. I would always end up sitting in the car because I couldn't stand watching them get drunk and act like they were eighteen again. Last summer Brad told me not to bother coming anymore. We'd had a fight about Manny Zimmerman.

"Manny is pathetic," I said to Brad. "He humiliates himself just so he can feel like one of the guys. And the truth is, you don't even like him. You think you're better than him."

"That's bullshit," Brad said. "You don't know what you're talking about."

Manny's the one who allegedly ate fifty eggs without throwing up, just like Paul Newman in *Cool Hand Luke*. That was long before I met him, but I'd heard the story at least half a dozen times. According to Brad, there were a hundred guys there, even some from neighbouring towns. And now Manny carries that ridiculous moment of glory around with him as if it was the peak of his life, that moment when someone stuffed the fiftieth egg in his mouth and everyone cheered.

"Every town has guys like Manny," I said. "They're stupid. They have no self-respect."

"You don't know anything about Manny," Brad said. "And don't bother coming next time. No one will miss you."

When Maryann phoned from her parents' place and asked me to drive down and stay with her for a few days, Brad got it into his head that I was going back for a weekend of good times. He wanted to come along, thought I was leaving him out.

"Why can't you understand?" I said to him. "It's not like you think. There's not going to be a party."

"Don't you want to show me the sights in your old home town?" he asked.

"No," I said, and that was that. He was hurt, but we didn't talk about it again.

The four-hour drive seemed to take all day. I watched the tail lights in front of me and wondered what Maryann would look like, if she'd still be the same, if I'd still be the same. Until then I'd tried not to think about it too much. I'd told Brad all the big things, showed him pictures of me and Maryann acting silly for the camera, showed him the high school year books, told him about my father. But I'd never encouraged him to ask questions about the little things, the details.

I watched the mileage. As I got closer I thought about my parents' house. I didn't know the people who bought it from my mother, a young couple, new in town. Maybe they've torn it down and built a new split-level, I thought. They hadn't, of course. You could see it outside Maryann's kitchen window, same colour, same fence, same lean on the back porch. I was relieved to see strangers in the yard.

Maryann had come on her own. Her Welsh husband and her daughter had stayed in England, I didn't ask why. We had two days to visit and we spent most of the time in the living room. It was strange, almost formal. Her mother brought us trays of food and we ate politely, not at all like the ravenous adolescent pups we used to be. I hadn't thought to bring any pictures of Brad with me, but Maryann had an album full of snapshots of her family. Her husband looked like a nice, comfortable Welshman with a wool sweater and a big smile. Her daughter looked just like her. She asked me if we were planning to have kids and I said yes. Her mother asked me what we were waiting for and said I was waiting for Brad to grow up. I meant it as a joke, but they both stared at me as though as I'd just confessed I'd married what my mother called a good-for-nothing. Maryann and I used to roll our eyes whenever my mother would warn us. "The worse thing that can happen to a girl is for her to marry a good-for-nothing."

The afternoon of my second day there, Maryann suggested that we go for a walk. I'd been standing at the kitchen window staring across the alley, thinking about my father building the playhouse for me, trying not to be sentimental.

"Let's," Maryann said. "I haven't been out the door since I got here."

It was a warm day for December and we walked from one end of town to the other. We didn't talk about memories, just stopped once in a while and looked at some landmark that meant the same thing to both of us. We passed the old hall. There was no trace of the fire, no trace of my father.

"I wonder what became of Dallas McMaster," I said. I remembered that at the trial he'd cried and said he hadn't meant to kill anybody.

"He's back in jail again, according to Mom," Maryann said. "He got really heavy into drugs when he was in the first time."

She hooked her arm in mine and we walked up to the highway, past the old fast food drive-in.

"No McDonald's yet," I said.

Maryann laughed. We were standing in the snow on the side of the highway and Maryann was laughing just the way she used to. I knew if I closed my eyes I would see us the way we were then. So I kept them open and said I was cold. We turned away from the drive-in and headed back to her parents' place.

That night as I lay in bed in the spare room I saw the fire, not the way it happened in the middle of town, but the way Maryann and I saw it from the gravel pit. And even though it was December, I threw back the covers on the bed. I could feel the heat. The heat of the June day rising off the pavement. The heat rising into the night sky.

The evening of the last day of school we were in Maryann's father's car, parked in the lot at the drive-in. It was practically deserted. There was a dance at the hall that night, but Maryann

91

and I weren't going. Maryann's boy friend Jeff was taking a younger woman, Catherine from grade ten. I wanted to go anyway but Maryann didn't, and she talked me into thinking we could find something else to do, something better, more exciting. It was typical of our friendship. Maryann made the decisions.

We sat in the car with the windows down and the radio turned up. There was a car next to us with two guys in it and they had their radio tuned to the same station. We ordered french fries and milkshakes and Maryann kept looking at the two guys.

"What do you think?" she asked me. "Should we strike up a conversation with them? They must be from somewhere else. I've never seen them before."

Strike up a conversation. Maryann was talking big. I had no idea how you went about doing that, and I didn't think she did either.

"Nice car, don't you think?" Maryann said to me.

"Yeah," I said, hoping they would drive away.

The carhop brought their tray and as she was leaving, the driver hollered after her for more ketchup.

"Did you hear his accent?" Maryann said to me. "I think he's French."

Maryann got out of the car and pretended to check the back tires. The two guys watched her. When she got back in, she reported to me that their car had Quebec licence plates. That did it, as far as she was concerned. There was nothing outstanding about the way either of them looked, but the accents suddenly made them exotic and desirable. Quebec was far away, more akin to France than it was to western Canada. A song came on the radio and Maryann sang along at the top of her lungs, giddy, showing off. The guys next to us sang too, so I awkwardly joined in and we had a quartet of voices. When the song was over, Maryann took the plunge.

"Hey," she called out. "Why don't you come and sit with us."

I looked away, out the window toward the highway, tried to concentrate on the summer smells, clover in the ditches. I couldn't have done it, but I was suddenly glad Maryann had.

One of them, the one with dark hair, was better looking than the other.

"I'm Gilles," he said, getting into the back seat with his milk-shake and burger. "That's Yvon." Yvon slammed the door. Close

92

up, you could see that his hair was stringy and hadn't been washed for a while. He had on a denim shirt with the sleeves rolled up, and I could see a little butterfly tattooed on his forearm.

"We're from Montreal," said Gilles with a very thick accent. "We're Québécois."

"No kidding," said Maryann. Everyone laughed.

"I was in Quebec once," I said, turning in my seat to look at the two in the back. "My family went to Expo. That was in Montreal."

"Big deal," said Yvon. "Big fucking deal."

Everyone laughed at that too. But what was the joke?

"Dana likes to go on little family holidays," Maryann said.

"Shut up, Maryann," I said, embarrassed.

"Don't get mad," said Maryann. "It's just a joke."

"Don't mind Yvon," Gilles said to me. "He thinks he's an anarchist but mostly he just hates everything."

What was an anarchist? Maryann seemed to know. At least she pretended she did.

"Do you girls go to high school?" Gilles asked.

"Nope," Maryann answered. "We're finished. Thank God for that. I couldn't stand this dump for another year. Next year we're going to university."

"University," said Yvon. "What a lot of bullshit." He pronounced it *boolsheet*. "I went there but I quit."

"He didn't quit," said Gilles. "They kicked him out. He failed everything and they told him not to come back next year."

"They couldn't teach me anything," said Yvon.

I wasn't sure what he was saying. I was excited about going to university. I knew Maryann was too.

"And what do you do?" Maryann asked Gilles. "Did they kick you out of university too?"

"Nah," said Gilles. "I work for my old man in Montreal. He gave me the summer off."

"His old man is rich," said Yvon. "Capitalista. Scum."

"Piss off," said Gilles. "He's not that bad."

When they finished eating, Gilles asked if there was anything exciting going on in town. I started to tell them about the dance, thinking it would be fairly impressive to show up with two guys from Quebec. Maryann interrupted me.

"Kids' stuff," she said. "Boring. Why don't we just drive around for a while. We'll show you the town."

93

"Wait for a minute," said Gilles. He jumped out of the car, rummaged in the back seat of his own car, and returned with his jacket rolled up under his arm.

"Okay," he said, climbing back in. "Drive on."

It's the laughter I remember most. We laughed at anything and everything. Gilles and Yvon cracked a lot of jokes about Saskatchewan being the ass end of the donkey and Maryann brazenly told pea soup jokes and talked in a silly French accent. She had Gilles and Yvon in stitches. I turned sideways in my seat and tried to get a good look at them. I could see that Gilles and Maryann were playing some kind of game with each other, bantering back and forth, sending out signals. I wasn't sure about Yvon. He may have been trying to catch my eye. I couldn't tell, but I smiled anyway just in case.

"Hey," he said. "You girls like to drink hard stuff?" He went through a pantomime then, tipping his head back, holding an invisible bottle to his lips and pretending to swallow, making his Adam's apple bounce up and down. I noticed big sweat marks under the arms of his denim shirt.

Maryann looked at me, asking if I was game. I gave her a look that could have meant one thing or the other. It was up to her. It was always up to her.

Yvon pulled an almost full bottle of rye out of Gilles' jacket.

"Sorry we don't have any dope," he said. "We smoked it all in northern Ontario. What an ugly place. Nothing but trees."

"You don't have to worry about that here," Maryann said. "This place is truly treeless."

More laughter.

"Truly treeless," Yvon said. "That's good. When we get back to Montreal we'll say, 'It's true, Saskatchewan is truly treeless.' "

Maryann laughed as if that was the funniest thing she'd ever heard. It did sound ridiculous, silly words mixed with the accent.

"Keep that bottle down," she said, heading west on the highway.

There was a place we used to go to drink along the creek on the edge of town. But Maryann didn't drive us there because she figured the cops would be around, being that it was the last day of school. She drove to the gravel pit instead. Not too scenic, but it was starting to get dark anyway.

The gravel pit was a strange place to be at dusk. It was eerie, a huge lot with the surface of the earth scraped away. We

94

parked at the foot of a heap of gravel and leaned our heads out
the windows into the warm air. There were lots of mosquitoes
but we left the windows down anyway and slapped and cursed.
We didn't have anything to mix with the rye so we just passed
the bottle.

"Hope you guys don't have any weird germs," Maryann said
when she took it. She was showing Gilles and Yvon a good time
and she was good at it.

"So," she said, taking a swig and passing the bottle to me.
"What are you guys going to do in Vancouver?"

"We've got some friends out there," Gilles said. "We're just
going to hang around for a while."

"We might even go to California or Mexico," said Yvon. "We're
going to have a good time. Get laid a lot and have a good time."
He took a hard swallow from the bottle, then handed it back
to me, wiping his mouth across the butterfly on his forearm.

I don't know what came over me. It was ridiculous, but I
thought I knew what he was talking about.

"Everybody," I said slowly, "should have a good time."

They all looked at me as if they were noticing for the first
time that I was there. Yvon stared, studying me.

"Hey Dana," he said. "You want to come with us? I've got lots
of room in my sleeping bag."

I was flattered. He had directed that at me, had really paid
attention to me, the way Gilles had been attentive to Maryann
all evening. I casually draped my arm across the back of the
seat and laughed his offer aside.

Someone decided we should go for a walk. There was nowhere
to go, so we climbed to the top of the gravel heap. Maryann
and I were both wearing sundresses and sandals. The gravel
was loose and we kept sliding back, skinning bare knees. I
wondered if the gravel was like a big pile of wheat; when we
got to the top we would be swallowed up, sucked down inside
and never seen again. I started to giggle, then sat down and
laughed hysterically.

"What's so funny?" It was Yvon. He sat down beside me. "I
want to have a good laugh too." I told him what was so funny.

"You are one strange girl," he said. I thought it was a com-
pliment. He took my arm and we climbed to the top together.

"We take our chances," he yelled when we were on the peak.
"We court death and have no fear. I piss into the sky."

95

I quickly turned my back as he reached for the fly of his jeans. I knew my laughter was loud and self-conscious, but I didn't want to hear the splash of his urine on the rocks. Maryann told me to be quiet.

"For God's sake," she said. "It isn't that funny."

Gilles and Maryann were sitting down. I could see that Gilles had his arm around Maryann's back. I sat down beside them. Yvon did up his fly and sat down too. The town lay before us in the distance, lit up like a summer carnival.

"You see that flashing red light?" Maryann said. She pointed to a neon sign on the edge of town. "It says *Motel*. It's not though. It's really the local whorehouse."

That wasn't true. As far as I knew, we didn't have a local whorehouse.

"Maybe we should stay here for a week or so, eh Gilles," Yvon said. "More fun than Vancouver, maybe."

Gilles and Maryann had the whiskey. They passed it around and that was the end of it. Yvon flung the empty bottle out into the night and we heard it smash on the rocks below.

I'm not sure exactly how long we were up there, but it must have been a few hours because we saw the fire. It didn't look like much, but for a brief time flames leapt into the darkness from somewhere in the centre of town.

"All right," said Yvon, slapping his thigh, jumping up. "A fire. Let's go and watch it."

"Nope," said Maryann. "Dana's father is a fireman. She can't show up at a fire pissed to the gills."

Yvon sat down again and the fire settled into a red glow. We guessed at what might be burning. Maryann decided it was somebody's garage. I thought it was more than likely a street fire, set by kids on the last day of school. That was kind of a tradition. You dragged a bunch of straw bales onto Main Street, lit them, then high-tailed it before you got caught. Within a few days everybody in town knew which kids did it because they couldn't keep their mouths shut, but nothing much was ever done. It occurred to me I might have a hard time sneaking into the house later; my father would probably still be up because of the fire.

"Come on, strange girl," Yvon said suddenly, grabbing my hand. "I'll race you to the bottom."

"You watch out for him," Maryann said to me as I stood up. "He's French." Then she practically fell over sideways laughing.

"For God's sake," I said. "It isn't that funny." A small triumph, but one that filled me with self-congratulation.

Getting down the gravel pile wasn't easy. I was drunk. The loose stones kept sliding out from under my feet and the darkness threw me. I couldn't tell where the bottom was.

"This is how you do it," said Yvon. He took off, running sideways down the steep slope, first one way, then the other, criss-crossing until he was down. I could hear the gravel echoing after him in miniature landslides. Then it was still.

"Come on," he called. "It's easy."

I could just make him out. He looked a long way off. I closed my eyes and ran, back and forth, down toward the figure at the bottom. It worked. At the foot of the heap I collapsed and gravel rained down on me. My shoes were full of little stones.

"That was very good," Yvon said, helping me up. He put his arm around me and we walked to the car. We climbed into the back seat and Yvon pulled the door shut. I took off my sandals and shook them out the open window. Yvon leaned over the front seat and turned the car key so the radio came on. Van Morrison sang and the words were for me.

> *Hey, where did we go days when the rains came*
> *Down in the hollow playin' a new game*
> *Laughing and a-running, hey, hey*
> *Skipping and a-jumping*
> *In the misty morning fog*
> *With our hearts a-thumping*
> *And you, my brown-eyed girl.*

Actually, Maryann was the brown-eyed girl. But just for a while I thought it might be me. Yvon was fun. He liked me. He moved across the seat toward me, put his arm around me, kissed me.

"So," he said. "Now we are alone and I think you're very attractive. I like your sense of humour."

It was black, no moon, and I couldn't see his face. I felt his hand on my breast. I pushed it away, kissing him at the same time. I didn't want him to stop kissing me.

"What's the matter," he said. "Don't you like me?"

"Sure," I said. "I like you a lot. You're different from the guys around here." I leaned against him, ran my hand up and down his arm. I tried to guess where the butterfly was, thought I could feel it, a spot where the skin was just a bit smoother than on the rest of his arm. I wondered what Maryann and Gilles were doing. I listened to the radio and the mosquitoes and the sporadic wailing of the sirens.

"Come on," he said, gently pushing my shoulders sideways and down. "I'll behave. I promise. I just want to kiss you."

So I let him push me down on the seat, and I let him lie on top of me. When he put his hands on my breasts again, I tried to get my own hands against his chest to push him away. But he was strong and I could feel the muscles tense in his arms. I panicked, twisting beneath him, trying to sit up. Suddenly I felt his teeth on my ear lobe.

"Cock-tease," he hissed, and he bit down hard. My eyes watered. "Please," I whispered, trying not to cry out. I didn't want Gilles and Maryann to hear. I was humiliated that this was happening. He didn't stop. He pushed my skirt up and roughly pulled my underpants down. It didn't take him long and I closed my eyes and tried to hold my breath. He kept his teeth on my ear lobe until he was done. The mosquitoes were all over my legs, but I lay very still and let them bite. I heard Maryann shrieking as she and Gilles came sliding toward the car.

Yvon quickly lifted himself off of me and I pulled my underwear up and straightened my skirt in the dark. Gilles got into the driver's seat and Maryann sat next to him.

"These girls from Saskatchewan are nice, eh Yvon," said Gilles. He put his arm around Maryann and she snuggled against him.

"Yeah," said Yvon. "They're nice. But I think we should hit the road. Get to Vancouver before September."

"Yeah," said Maryann. "It's late. We have to get home."

We didn't talk much on the way back to town. Maryann let Gilles drive and she leaned her head back and sang along with the radio. The drive-in was closed when we got there. Gilles' car was the only one on the lot.

"Have fun in Vancouver," Maryann said to them.

"We will," said Gilles. Yvon didn't say anything, just got out and slammed the door without even looking at me. I got in the front with Maryann. Gilles and Yvon had a little argument about who was going to drive and who was going to sleep, then Gilles got into the driver's seat. Both cars backed out, one going one direction, one the other. The two cars passed, and Maryann waved madly.

"Stop the car," I said to her. She did, and Gilles backed up, then stopped beside us. The car windows were down. I looked across Maryann and Gilles to see Yvon glaring at me as though he was defying me to say something. I don't know what I was expecting, remorse maybe, but not defiance.

"Never mind," I said, "let's just get going."

Maryann put the car in drive and stepped on the gas.

"You're acting weird," she said to me. "I don't think you hold your liquor very well."

"Fuck off, Maryann," I said, not feeling weird, just pathetic. "Fuck off and drive me home."

The house was empty. I went to bed, then got up again because it was strange that no one was home. I sat by myself in the living room and wondered what was going on.

Maryann's parents brought my mother home from the hospital just after one o'clock. We'd been right about the fire. It hadn't amounted to much and they were able to put it out fairly quickly. It had started in the hall a few minutes after eleven. Dallas McMaster and three of his friends had been kicked out of the dance for drinking. The front of the hall was decorated with paper lanterns and Dallas went back inside and lit them on fire. Everybody cleared out the back door.

The fire truck was there in no time, just as it was supposed to be. My father climbed up on the roof to hose the fire from above. He slipped on the roof and fell off.

The spare bedroom in Maryann's mother's house was cold. I woke shivering in the early morning and was glad to get up and dress. I went to the window. The winter sky was clear. I'd been planning to load my bag and head back to the city, but I decided to call Brad instead and ask him to drive down. We spent most of the afternoon with Maryann and her mother, then went out for a walk. I took him to the hall and told him the whole story, Maryann, Yvon, my father, everything. I told him not to talk, just to listen. After supper we headed out in separate cars for the city. We drove all the way without stopping. I tried not to think about the fire. I thought about Brad and his friends and their good times. I thought about Manny Zimmerman. Maybe his good times were more than a little like mine. Maybe he puked his guts out after eating all those eggs, even if no one saw him do it.

HOW I DIDN'T
KILL WALLY EVEN
THOUGH HE DESERVES IT

What I'm doing right now is tying Wally up, wrapping the
rope around and around, and him screaming and kicking and
hurling abuses at me something awful. The rope is the one we
use to tie the furniture down in the back of the half-ton every
time we move. Which is pretty often. Maybe you haven't noticed
that someone is helping me. She's so small you have to look two
or three times to even notice she's there. Have a close look down
by Wally's foot, the left one. She's no more than three and a
half inches tall. And you know, it's the funniest thing. You can
see for yourself how big and downright mean Wally is. A real
bruiser. And you can see I'm nowhere near his size, even if I
have put on a few pounds in the last ten years. But with that
little slip of a thing down there hanging onto Wally's toe, I don't
seem to be having any trouble at all wrapping him up so he can't
harm anyone, especially me. And it's going to be a piece of cake
getting him into the closet and closing the door. Hard to believe,
I know, but it's true. He can fight and holler and curse all he
wants, but I'm not letting him out until he learns a thing or
two. That's just the way it is and I know I'm doing the right
thing. I can feel it.

This whole business started when I decided I was going to
kill Wally. I really was. I was sick and tired of him being mean
and ugly. A body can only take so much. And I figured I had
nothing to lose. The only thing I've got to be thankful for in
my life is that we never had any kids, and what kind of a blessing
is that?

I thought about how to kill Wally and the only thing I could
come up with was a good solid knock on the head. Looking back,
that doesn't seem like such a smart idea. Wally's head is like

a blacksmith's anvil. I doubt that I could have done much more than make him madder than he is most of the time already. It's a good thing she came along and put a stop to things. Lord knows what he would have done to me.

Anyway, there I was, all set to stand on a chair by the door and knock Wally on the head with his own fourteen-pound post maul. I knew he'd be home any minute and I was going to lift that maul into the air and bring it down on his head. Driven him right into the floor, that's what I'd liked to have done. Driven him right through the basement ceiling and into the cement, never to be heard from again.

I was doing a little practicing, trying to get the maul up over my head, standing on the chair, weaving around, doing a sort of dance to keep my balance, when I heard this voice. A little one, mind you, but a voice all the same.

"And just what, pray tell, is going on here?" the voice said. "A savage killing in the planning stages is what it looks like to me."

What do you do when something like that happens? I can tell you. It crosses your mind that maybe you're going crazy. It occurred to me that Wally and his thirty years of bad treatment had finally driven me over the edge. I lowered the post maul and stood there on the chair shaking like a leaf and sweating. And then it hit me. Conscience, that's what it was. It was my conscience talking.

"Oh no you don't," I said, lifting the maul. "I don't want to hear from you at all. I don't care if what I've got planned here is wrong or right. I don't give a damn one way or the other. I'm going to kill that bastard Wally and then my troubles will be over."

"What about the Ten Commandments?" the voice said. "What about the Golden Rule?"

"I don't care about any of that," I said. "All I care about is that Wally gets what he deserves."

I had managed to lift the maul up over my head and was just about to swing it down to get the feel of it, when all of a sudden the fourteen pounds felt like four hundred pounds. I could feel myself going over backwards and the only thing to do was to let go of the maul and try to get my balance. It landed on the floor and didn't seem to do any damage. I climbed down to pick it up again, thinking that Wally would be home any minute and find me with the post maul in the living room and how would I explain that? By this time I was sick and tired of this conscience business. I had a gruesome job to do and I wanted to be done with it.

I bent over to pick up the maul and there she was, sitting on the end of it, not much bigger than my thumb. She was dressed in a turquoise blue jogging suit and miniature running shoes. Cute as a button, was my first reaction, just what any little girl would like to find under the Christmas tree.

"How do you like them apples, sister?" she said, and I tell you, my blood pressure shot up past the red line in two seconds flat. I forgot all about Christmas and jogging suits and thought, nobody's supposed to be able to *see* their conscience. Not even someone who's about to pound her husband's head down to his kneecaps.

"You can't just up and kill somebody whenever you get the notion," she said, shaking her finger at me.

I thought about Wally and felt myself getting cocky in spite of the situation.

"Why not?" I flashed at her. "The bastard has tried to kill me any number of times. It's time he got some of his own. I can't think of anything else that will smarten him up." I paused, proud of myself. "And just who exactly are you anyway? The good fairy?"

She didn't bat an eyelash (not that I could have seen it if she had), she just sat and swung her legs and beckoned for me to get closer. I squatted down.

"Never mind who I am," she said. "All you need to know is that I'm here to save you from yourself. You're a dangerous woman."

"Oh, am I?" I said. "Is that why I walk around with these bruises?" (I lifted up my dress and showed her a big ugly one on my thigh.) "Is that why I had to get false teeth twenty years ago after Wally knocked out most of my real ones? Is that why my shoulders ache when I lie in bed at night so I have to get up and take a painkiller to get to sleep? Oh yeah," I said, "I'm a dangerous woman all right. Real dangerous. I think that bastard Wally needs someone to protect him from me."

And it was the funniest thing. She stopped swinging her white joggers and her eyes (big green ones) filled with tears.

"It's not Wally I'm worried about," she said. "It's you."

I didn't know what to do. I just squatted there and she cried and finally I said, "Well. There's no sense crying over me. I've been living like this too many years and I quit crying about it a long time ago. Now if you'll kindly move, I'll finish the job and be done with it." I tried to stand up but I'd stayed in the same position too long. I had to unbend myself one leg at a time, like a fold-up card table. It kind of took the wind out of my sails. Still, I was determined. It was too late to turn back and I really didn't give a damn about myself or Wally or anyone else.

After I'd given my back a good stretch I bent over again to pick up the maul, planning to shake the little thing off. She was gone. I'm cracking up, I thought. A few bricks short, as Wally would say. He's driven me to this. He deserves what he's going to get. I gripped the wooden handle of the maul. Wally was coming. I could see him out the front-room window, weaving down the street like a drunken sailor.

"Oh no you don't," the voice said from somewhere behind me. And then I felt something sharp sink into my right ankle. It was her, and she had latched onto me with her teeth. I screamed and she let go.

"Into the closet with you," she said, and darted back and forth between one ankle and the other.

"Stop that," I said, kicking at her. "Stop that right now. He's coming. I have to get ready."

"Into the closet," she said, biting my left ankle like one of those chihuahua dogs that fit into a tea cup. "Get moving. Quickly, quickly." She was so fast I couldn't get at her. I could see now why she wore the running shoes. I was moving toward the closet, trying to avoid her teeth and kicking at her as I went. Before I knew it the doorway was in front of me and then I was inside and something was in my mouth so I couldn't yell. I could feel a rope going around and around me until I couldn't move.

"There," she said, and then I heard Wally coming in the front door. He slammed it behind him.

"What the hell," I heard him say. I pictured him in the living room, drunk and ugly. "Hey," he yelled. "What's this post maul doing here?" Silence. I felt my blood pressure going up again. "It damn well better be gone by the time I'm back down here." I heard him tramping up the stairs to the bathroom. "Do you hear me?" he called from the top of the stairs. Silence. "And you damn well better answer me next time I ask you a question."

HOW I DIDN'T KILL WALLY

I heard him stomp down the hallway and slam the bathroom door.

I don't know what happened to the post maul. It disappeared and I haven't seen it since. I lay scrunched up in the closet for a long time, scared, wondering what Wally would do when I didn't show up.

I must have fallen asleep, and when I woke up it was morning and the ropes were gone. I went to the kitchen and made Wally his breakfast. He came downstairs and fixed himself a tomato juice with four aspirins and a raw egg mixed into it, which is his own special cure for a hangover. I waited for him to ask me where I'd been, but he didn't say anything. When I placed a plate of bacon and eggs in front of him he slapped it across the table. I managed to catch it before it landed on the floor, which is better than some mornings around here. I took it that he was too hungover to eat so I scraped the eggs into the garbage and headed down into the basement to busy myself with sorting the laundry in order not to be in Wally's road. I felt let down. All my enthusiasm for bashing Wally was gone and I didn't think about killing him again for a long time.

It was the potatoes that did it. I had worked hard, weeding and hoeing, hilling, picking off potato beetles by hand. I figured that maybe we'd been in one place long enough for me to do something homey, build a bin in the basement and keep potatoes all winter like my mother used to. I figured Wally might even like that. So I dug up a space in the back yard, bought seed potatoes with the grocery money, and went to work.

It was early August, just about the time you can start robbing potato hills and have those first meals served up with lots of real butter. The skins on the potatoes are so thin then that you don't even have to peel them. I was feeling good, like maybe I could start calling this little town home. I'd even had a few conversations with Crazy Florence next door, as though we were real neighbours.

I was out in the back yard, digging around in the hills with my bare hands, trying to guess how many potatoes would be in each hill and how big they'd be by the end of September. And what should Wally do but back the half-ton into the yard as close as he could to the back door. I knew what that meant, I'd seen it too many times before. Pretty soon he'd be carrying out dishes and chairs and blankets and loading them all into the back of that truck.

"Wally," I said as he stepped out of the cab. "Just what are you fixing to do? Don't tell me we're off again. Don't tell me you've gone and got yourself fired and we're heading down the road to some other town where I don't know a soul and nobody knows me nor cares to either. Don't tell me that, Wally. I couldn't bear to hear it."

Wally just grunted and slammed the screen door to the house and I knew that was exactly where we were headed. I followed him up the steps and hollered in the door.

"And what about my potatoes, Wally? What do you expect me to do about this patch of perfectly good potatoes? Leave them here for total strangers? Maybe people who don't care about fresh potatoes? Maybe people who will leave them in the ground to freeze and rot? Tell me Wally, if we leave this place what do you expect me to do about these potatoes?"

I heard him coming and I thought maybe I had gone a little too far. I was not usually inclined to speak to Wally like that. I tended to go along with him, watch him load up the truck and get in beside him without saying much at all. I thought he might hit me, but he just stormed out the door, pushing me out of his way, and leaped into the cab.

"What am I going to do about the potatoes?" he said starting up the truck. "What am I going to do?" he said, grinding the gears as he slammed it into reverse. And then I knew what he was going to do and there was nothing I could do to stop him. I stood on the step as he drove back and forth over the potato patch and spun the tires and threw dirt and potatoes all over the yard. I watched him and I thought, I'm going to kill him. I don't know how I'm going to do it, but I'm going to kill him. I sat down on the steps and hatched a plan right then and there. And I wasn't going to let my conscience get the best of me this time either.

I knew a little bit about explosives. And I was pretty sure Wally had some dynamite stored in the garage. I would wire up his truck and when he got in it to drive off, bango, no more Wally.

I needed a few supplies to carry out my plan. I went into the house and got the grocery money from my apron pocket while

Wally was still digging up my potato patch. I headed out the front door and walked to the hardware store.

"Doing a bit of blasting?" Mr. Ferguson asked as he rang up my purchases.

"We've got a terrible big rock right in the middle of my garden," I said.

I stopped at the IGA for bread and milk so Wally wouldn't be suspicious. When I got home the potato patch was ruined. Wally was still sitting in the truck, listening to the radio. I fixed him three fried egg sandwiches and opened two beers and set them on the table.

"Wally," I called out the back door. "I've fixed you a little lunch. Fried egg sandwiches. And beer. Two of them."

He took the bait. He turned off the truck and stomped into the kitchen. He looked me in the eye and I looked him right back, trying not to give anything away.

"So that's what I think of your goddamned potatoes," he said.

"That's fine, Wally dear," I said. "I realize that I can't take them with me and that's all there is to it. You did the right thing. Now just enjoy your lunch and have a nap afterward if you want. I'll start packing up things in the living room."

I saw him eyeing the sandwiches like he was looking for poison and that gave me an idea for next time if the dynamite didn't work.

I took my bag of supplies and quietly went out the front door and around the side of the house to the garage. I found the dynamite hidden under a canvas tarp along with some other stuff Wally had brought home from work.

The truck was parked in the middle of the potato patch and I knew Wally couldn't see me from the kitchen. I crawled in and lay on the seat, figuring I could get the job done easy before Wally came back outside. Three sandwiches and two beers were usually enough to put him out for a couple of hours. I sang as I worked, really enjoying myself.

Oh, what a beautiful mornin'
Oh, what a beautiful day

I was just putting on the finishing touches when I heard the voice, singing along with me.

I've got a beautiful feelin'
Ev'rything's goin' my way.

I stopped singing. She hopped up onto the dash.

"I can see you're up to your old tricks again, sister," she said. "I thought you had learned your lesson."

I sat up and stared at her. I reached out my index finger and touched her to see if she was really there. I pinched myself to make sure I was awake and I pulled my hair at the back of my neck, where it really hurts, just to double check. I was awake and she was really there.

"You just stay out of this," I said to her. "I had enough of you last time. This is none of your business."

"Oh, but it is," she said. "Like I said before, I'm here to protect you from yourself." She looked toward the house. "What's he done this time?"

"What's he done this time?" I said. "Can't you see for yourself? Just have a look around. Just have a look at my potato patch and then ask what's he done this time. This is the last straw, I tell you. A body can only take so much and then she has to do something."

She peered through the windshield and checked out the potato patch.

"He really is bad news," she said. "There's no doubt about it."

She paused. I noticed that she was wearing a different jogging suit from the one she had on last time. This one was yellow with bold black stripes. She leaned forward and looked into my eyes.

"Now I want you to think about something," she said.

"Okay," I heard myself say. "I'll think about it."

"You've blown Wally into little pieces," she said. "A million of them. The police come screaming up to your house. Four, five, maybe even six police cars. Men, big bruisers, surround you and they all have their gun barrels pointed at your head. You look for sympathy, but you don't get any because they think you've just blown up one of their own. They take you away and all the neighbours are watching over their fences. They shake their heads and say, 'Well, we won't be seeing her again. She'll be locked up for life, even if he did deserve it.'"

I thought about it. It was like a moving picture in my head. Tut tut, too bad, they were all saying. Mrs. Bidwell across the street. Crazy Florence next door. Even the postman. Their voices were a low hum, getting louder and louder, coming from all around the truck. Tut tut, too bad.

The yellow jogging suit on the dash of the truck joined in. I blinked and she was doing deep knee bends. Tut tut, too bad.

Up down, up down. I was going mad; I had to be. A person's conscience never does deep knee bends.

"Stop," I yelled. I opened the door of the truck, jumped out and ran for the house. "I don't want to go to jail," I screamed, covering my ears with my hands.

There was an explosion from behind me. I was thrown onto my knees at the foot of the back steps. When I looked up, the truck was a mass of flames and Wally was gazing through the screen door.

"What the hell happened to my truck?" he said.

I stood up and wiped the dust off my knees, wondering what he would throw at me, wondering if I could make it over Florence's fence in time.

"I hope it's totalled," he said. "It's about time I got a new truck." He went back to the kitchen to finish his beer.

We didn't move. Wally couldn't get insurance for the truck because he had a $500 deductible and the truck wasn't worth that much. He tried to pay a couple of garage owners to say it was worth more, but they wouldn't do it. He managed to get some unemployment insurance by sending me to beg his ex-boss to say he had laid Wally off. But things were worse than ever because Wally was home all the time, calling me names, yelling at me and shoving me around for no reason, leaving empty beer bottles all over, snoring on the couch while I was trying to watch my programs on TV.

I started to forget about jail and think about poison. I figured the hardware store would be a good place to get rat bait.

"How'd the blasting go?" Mr. Ferguson asked me.

"Just fine," I said. "We blasted that rock with no trouble at all."

"So," Mr. Ferguson went on, "I hear Wally's had a little trouble with his truck."

"Funny thing, that was," I said.

"So," he said, busy straightening things on the counter. "Did Wally manage to get any insurance money?"

"None at all," I said trying to look grave.

Mr. Ferguson shook his head. "Some guys have all the luck," he said.

"Do you have any rat bait?" I asked. "We've got more trouble with rodents than you'd care to think about."

He directed me to the right aisle, and there she was on the shelf right next to the boxes of poison. Just sitting there in her coal black jogging suit with the hood up, looking mournful as you could imagine. A good act, I thought. Well, I wasn't going to let it get to me.

"You again," I said. "Well, you can't talk me out of it this time. My mind's made up. I'm going through with it."

I put my hand on the box, which had a picture of a dead rat with crosses on its eyes. She still didn't say anything, and I got the feeling she wasn't planning to. She looked so defeated I all of a sudden thought I would cry.

"Did you say something?" Mr. Ferguson called from behind the counter. "Finding what you need?"

"Yes, thanks," I called, my voice sounding hoarser than I wanted it to. I looked the woman in the eye. "Aren't you going to try to talk me out of it?" I said.

She shook her head.

"Why not?" I asked.

She didn't say anything, but she looked so miserable that I wondered if she'd buy some poison for herself.

It was the funniest thing. I couldn't bring myself to pick up that box of rat bait. I knew I was feeling low because I had her feeling so low. And I was beginning to figure out that I liked her. I wanted to make her happy. I tried an experiment by moving my hand away from the box. She brightened up as if someone had just lit a candle in her heart. And I felt that way too, as if someone had lit a candle in my heart.

"I guess today's not the day," I said. "I guess I'll go on home and make Wally his pork chops just like I do every Tuesday, and I won't be putting any poison in them either."

"Good for you," she shouted, jumping up. "Now we're getting somewhere."

"You might be getting somewhere," I said, leaving the store empty-handed. "I'm just on my way home to get yelled at and knocked around the house a few times, same old story. If that's getting somewhere, I don't know anything."

"Just don't be so sure," the woman said. "I still have a trick or two up my sleeve."

So. Wally didn't die by rat bait and that brings me to where we are now. Me and this little bit of a thing tying Wally up in the closet. I'm wearing a fuchsia jogging suit just like hers. I found it in the mailbox this morning, wrapped in silver paper.

"So what do you think of them apples?" I say to Wally when we have him tied up good, a sock stuffed in his mouth so he can't yell. "How do you feel now, big boy?" I say. He jerks his feet around a bit. "Things are going to change around this place," I tell him, "and I'll just be leaving you in here for a while to mull things over." I close the closet door, then open it again. "And we're not moving away from here either," I add.

The two of us, in our fuchsia jogging suits, sit on the couch watching *The Lives of Others* on TV and eating popcorn.

"These people are disgusting," I say.

She nods. She's working on a single white puff the size of her head.

"They have no morals," I say, suddenly depressed about the *real* state of things.

She agrees.

"What will we do if it doesn't work?" I ask. "What if he's worse than ever when we let him out?"

"Shhhhhhh," she says. "Just watch this."

On TV, Mandy is blow-drying her hair in front of the bathroom mirror. Lance is singing in the bathtub, scrubbing his back the way people do on TV. Mandy keeps looking at him and moving closer to the bathtub. Suddenly she tosses the dryer into the tub with Lance. He screams. The program cuts to a big yellow box of Sunlight detergent.

"Electrocution?" I ask her, my mouth full of popcorn.

She lowers the white puff of corn to her lap and grins.

SUKIE

Maggie stood outside the salon door for a minute before she opened it. Aldo's car was parked in front, a 1967 Stingray, white, in mint condition. It was parked on an angle, taking up two spaces so people couldn't bang the sides when they opened their car doors carelessly. Why couldn't she have done something like that for Sukie, Maggie thought. Something to keep her safe. Maggie looked at the Stingray, protected by layers of shiny acrylic and Aldo's careful parking. A wet snow was falling and the flakes seemed to hit the car and slide right off.

Now that she was there, Maggie was afraid to go inside. No one else that she knew came to Aldo, but you could never count on being completely anonymous. She'd already faced her close friends, people who'd come by the house, but she wasn't ready yet for those other awkward meetings. She told herself that she would act as though nothing was wrong. People wouldn't say anything unless they were forced to and she would not encourage them. She was pretty sure Aldo wouldn't know. It wasn't the kind of thing that's reported in the paper, not like someone getting thrown off a motorcycle or a window washer falling ten stories to the pavement. Even if Aldo had seen Sukie's death notice in the paper, he wouldn't have recognized the name. Salina Escott, it had read. Salina was her real name, the one Maggie had given her. Sukie was something her father had come up with when she was a little girl.

Maggie opened the salon door and stepped inside. The brass bells hanging on the inside of the door rang and Maggie smelled the perm solution and perfumed hairspray.

"How are you today, Maggie?" Aldo called as she was shaking the snow off her coat. Good, Maggie thought. He doesn't know.

The greeting had been easy and familiar, not the words of someone who didn't know what to say.

Aldo was spraying the finishing touches on a pink mousse job. The girl in his chair was no more than thirteen or fourteen. She didn't look at all like Sukie had at that age, but still Maggie's first inclination was to look away. She couldn't bear being around young girls, didn't even like to see them on the street, but she knew she couldn't keep that up forever. She forced herself to stare at the girl. It's okay to stare, she thought. They like it. That's why they do it. For attention. She noticed the girl had red plastic earrings that looked like giant safety pins. Aldo always took Maggie's earrings out when he cut her hair. Gently. One at a time. Then he would hand them to her and she would hold them under the plastic apron until he was finished. Maggie tried to think back to the first time he did that. She couldn't remember how it got started.

Maggie was sure Aldo didn't know about Sukie. He wouldn't have asked her how she was if he did. She watched him flip spiky pieces of the pink hair down over the girl's forehead. He would have given her some clue. A different kind of look. Anyway, how could he know? Maggie wasn't anybody important, she wasn't a part of any social circle that people talked about in hairdressers' shops. If she were the wife of a big lawyer in town, word might have gotten around.

Maggie hung her coat up with the others on the rack and slipped her boots off. She didn't bother checking in at the desk, the stylists all knew her. Ever since they'd moved here five years ago she'd been coming to Aldo. She'd discovered him by going through the yellow pages in the phone book and finding the salon closest to the house. The name, "Aldo's Hair Design", had made her a little nervous. She'd tried to talk Sukie into going with her, but she'd looked disgusted and said she couldn't possibly go to anyone without a recommendation. At sixteen Sukie had said that. How in the world had she developed such ideas at sixteen? She ended up going to someone that one of the girls at school told her about.

Maggie sat in a chair by the window and waited for Lisa to call her for her shampoo. Maggie hated washing her own hair and always had. When she was first married, Jack would wash it for her. He had been tender and told her how much he liked to do it. They even made love sometimes afterward. But washing her hair eventually became a chore for him and he let her know it. Still, she continued to ask him. "Jack, I absolutely have to wash my hair tonight," she would say, and he would throw his newspaper down on the couch and sullenly follow her to the bathroom. Once he said to her, "Why don't you just go out and get your hair done like other women?" She was hurt. She was afraid it meant he didn't love her anymore. Well, as it turned out, that was true.

Now she enjoyed going out to have her hair done. She wasn't even embarrassed anymore when Aldo asked her if she'd tried some hair product she'd never heard of that was sure to make her hair softer and shinier. The first time she'd been insulted, as though he was telling her she should do something about that horrible mess on her head. Now she took it as sign that she was part of whatever it was that went on in hair salons. She still wasn't like Sukie though, dependent on bottles of every kind of cosmetic under the sun. She didn't know what made Sukie the way she was. She had certainly been told enough that she was a beautiful young woman, too many times for her own good, Maggie thought. She had started worrying about wrinkles when she was still a child, no more than twelve or thirteen. Maggie remembered the violent temper tantrums about her hair before school in the morning. She broke the bathroom mirror once when she threw her brush at it.

Maggie heard a voice. "How are you today, Mrs. Escott?" It was Lisa, speaking to her from over the reception counter. She didn't wait for Maggie to answer. "Aldo will be with you in a minute," she said and quickly turned away.

Aldo would be washing her hair today? But why? That wasn't what usually happened. For a brief moment she panicked, thinking that something was wrong, maybe they knew after all. Then she told herself that was ridiculous, there would be a perfectly good reason for Aldo washing her hair which she would see if she'd just look around.

Maggie forced herself to take in the whole shop, the row of mirrors and chairs and hair dryers. It wasn't overly busy, one of the other stylists was sitting at her own chair having a cup of coffee. There were two ladies under the dryers, two more at the sinks, the young girl in Aldo's chair. Two other women were waiting next to Maggie, thumbing through hairstyle magazines. Still, Maggie didn't think Aldo had ever washed her hair. She would remember if he had. She looked at the clock on the wall. Twelve thirty. It was probably Lisa's lunch hour. There. It made sense.

Maggie watched as Aldo held a hand mirror for the girl in his chair. She posed, obviously in love with her rock video make-over. The girl paid at the counter and put on her coat. She kept glancing over her shoulder into the row of mirrors, smiling, completely self-satisfied. Sukie had never been satisfied like that. She would come home from a hair appointment, get in the shower, and wash it all out.

"Maggie?" It was Aldo speaking to her. "I can take you now."

Maggie lay back over the sink and closed her eyes. She felt the warm water on her scalp, just the right temperature. It felt wonderful. She lay there and let Aldo work the suds through her hair with his fingertips. She tried to decide if his hands felt different from Lisa's. Aldo, she decided, was a bit more attentive in his touch. He was being so careful not to let a drop of water run down her forehead. It was amazing, Maggie thought, how they never got soap in your eyes. When she washed her hair at home, she practically had to change her clothes afterward; she ended up with soap and water everywhere. Maggie suddenly became embarrassed at the closeness.

"Okay," Aldo said, wrapping a towel around her head. "Finished." He walked over to his chair and Maggie followed him. She sat and Aldo clipped the apron around her neck.

"And what are we planning to have done today?"

Maggie didn't know. She hadn't really thought about it. But the thought of having the same old thing — short, practical, easy to care for — made her cringe.

"Something new," she said. "Something completely different."

Aldo nodded. "A change is good for people," he said. "Women should change their hair styles every two years."

"Yes," Maggie said. "That's what I've been thinking." She paused. "I've been thinking about colour."

She hadn't really. The idea had just popped into her head that minute, maybe because as she looked at herself in the mirror, her wet hair making her look unattractive even by her standards, she could see the grey all along her hairline.

"Lots of women are letting their hair grey naturally," Aldo said. "There's a whole new attitude. Are you sure you want to colour it?"

"Yes," Maggie said. "I most definitely want to colour it." She could imagine herself in the mirror with no grey, younger. Aldo dyed his hair. She was sure of it. "Auburn," she said. "Yes. I want auburn."

She watched Aldo in the mirror. His hair was black, long on top and combed straight back. She didn't know how old he was. Her age, probably. Maybe five years younger. She wanted to ask him, but she would never do that. He knew she was divorced. Maggie knew what he would think if she asked him a personal question.

She could tell he didn't want to colour her hair. He was hesitating, thinking, running his fingers through her hair, studying it. The silence made her less sure.

"No," Aldo finally said. "I'll be perfectly honest. I don't think auburn would do a lot for you."

"What then?" she said, looking at him in the mirror. Did her voice have a slight waver? She didn't think so. She sat up straighter in the chair, checked herself in the mirror. She was composed, her expression the same as the one she'd rehearsed at home. She didn't want to give anything away.

She became conscious of Aldo's hands. Probing her scalp, moving bits of hair around her face, curling it on her cheek, then combing it all back with his fingers. They were in the mirror together, framed with frosted white light bulbs, like celebrities in their dressing room.

Sukie had wanted to be a celebrity. When she was in high school she told people she was going to be a model and move to Paris or New York. She tacked pictures of famous models all over her bedroom, women like Julianne Phillips and Christie Brinkley. "I could look like that," she used to say, studying them, studying herself for hours in her full-length mirror. Finally, in exasperation Maggie told her if she went to New York she'd probably end up waiting tables in some low-life bar and grill. She told her she was good-looking, yes, but it took more than looks to compete in that world. Maggie didn't even know if what she said was true, but she'd felt she had to get such nonsense out of Sukie's head. Sukie continued to pin up pictures of beautiful women, but Maggie didn't hear any more about modelling.

Aldo was speaking to her. "You should try a style," he was saying, "that sweeps your hair back and up." He demonstrated, gently lifting her hair back with his fingers. "You see?" he asked.

"It draws attention to your eyes. Your eyes are one of your strong points, you know."

She didn't know. She had never thought she had any strong points. She looked at her eyes then, studied them in the mirror. Perhaps they were. They were brown, unusually dark. Sukie had gotten her eyes from Maggie's side of the family. Maggie trembled.

"What about colour?" she asked, controlling her voice. "I do want colour. I've decided I definitely want colour."

Really, she wasn't at all decided. But change seemed important now that she'd thought about it. It was a way out of the darkness in her life. She needed a new look. And she would leave here with her new look, take a cab straight to the boutique section of the city and buy herself a new outfit. Something casual, something that would have made Sukie proud. Cocktail pants, perhaps, with a long top. Something bright. She could wear bright colours. One of Sukie's friends from Eaton's, a colour consultant, had told her she should wear bright colours. Maggie had scoffed, saying that colour-coding was all nonsense, just a way for people to make money. But now she would take Sukie's friend's advice.

"Mousse," Aldo said. "How about if we try coloured mousse? I have it in henna." He lifted the hair on the side of her head and spoke to her reflection. "I'll cut your hair so we can sweep it up on the sides. I'll show you how to use the mousse and if you don't like it you can wash it out."

Maggie looked at him, surprised. Could she really use mousse? She thought it was just for young people. For Sukie and her friends, for the girl with pink hair.

"Fine," she said, trying not to look too pleased. "I can try the colour and see how I like it. Good idea."

Aldo nodded. He unhooked the gold hoops in her ears and handed them to her. She looked down so their eyes wouldn't meet in the mirror, slipped her hand back under the plastic.

Maggie closed her eyes and thought about Sukie. She could see her behind the cosmetic counter in Eaton's. She looked like a nurse or a doctor in her white smock. That was part of the advertising, Maggie supposed. To make the whole show look clinical. Sukie had loved all that stuff that came in expensive coloured boxes, had used it faithfully since she started working there at eighteen. She had filled the bathroom shelves at home with rows and rows of bottles in all different sizes. Maggie had wanted her to go to university.

For some reason, Maggie remembered the Christmas she and Sukie flew to Toronto to visit her sister. Sukie had been about fifteen. In the Toronto airport, a strange man with a camera around his neck approached Maggie and asked her if he could marry Sukie. Maggie had been horrified, told the man certainly not and please leave them alone. The man began taking pictures of Sukie. Sukie was ecstatic and posed for him, even though Maggie told her to stop it and shouted at the man to go away. He left only after Maggie threatened to call the police. When a cab pulled up moments later, Sukie got in the back and slammed the door. Maggie sat next to the cab driver.

As Maggie thought about these things, the cosmetic counter with Sukie behind it kept coming back to her. Sukie with her thick bobbed hair. Sukie with her full mouth and cranberry coloured lipstick. Sukie showing women how to use the little chart on the counter to figure out their skin type and what colour group they should choose their makeup from. Maggie had never paid much attention. Why hadn't she? Perhaps she would go to Eaton's after she did the boutiques. Perhaps she would let whoever was behind the counter show her how to use the chart.

"Maggie?" It was Aldo's voice. "Maggie? Are you all right?"

She opened her eyes and saw herself in the mirror. She looked terrible. She was crying.

"I'm sorry," she said. "I didn't know." What should she tell him? She had decided before she came that she would not tell him. She'd thought she could come here and be Maggie with a beautiful daughter who worked at Eaton's. Not Maggie the failure, Maggie to be pitied.

"I was thinking," was all she could come up with to say.

Aldo handed her a kleenex from a box on the counter.

"I've almost finished cutting," he said. "Maybe we can forget about styling for today."

"Yes," Maggie said, squeezing her earrings until her fingernails dug into her hands. "I'll come back next week. I don't know what's wrong with me."

What would he think, Maggie wondered. He would probably think she was a neurotic divorced woman. She wondered why men didn't have to deal with that. Aldo was separated and no one thought he was lonely and neurotic. Maggie didn't anyway. He looked perfectly confident standing there in front of the mirror, talking to women, making suggestions for how they should change themselves.

Aldo quickly dried Maggie's hair and she got out of the chair without looking at herself in the mirror. She wrote Aldo a cheque, and took her coat from the rack. She accidently took someone else's first, then noticed her mistake and replaced it, searching blindly for her own. As she was putting it on, she noticed Lisa was watching her from the doorway to the back room. When their eyes met, Lisa stepped through and came to her.

"I'm sorry," Lisa said. Her voice shook. "I'm so sorry about your daughter." Then she turned and hurried to the back again.

Maggie sat down in a chair. She sat there with her coat half on and half off and stared after Lisa. They knew. They all knew. She sat there, staring, and finally Aldo came and helped her put her coat on. She shoved her gold earrings into her pocket. Aldo was going to drive her home. She knew it. He'd asked before if he could drive her home but she'd always said no. He took his leather jacket off the hanger and led her outside to his 1967 Stingray without saying a word. He manoeuvered the car out of the parking lot and onto the expressway. Maggie's hands lay limp and empty on top of her fur coat.

"I should have seen it coming," she said.

"Maybe," Aldo said. "Even so, sometimes you can't do a damn thing."

Maggie closed her eyes.

"As long as you know that," Aldo said.

FINE BONE CHINA

The street on which I live is lined with a double row of elm trees. Most summers they form a giant canopy over the sidewalks and houses, a kind of umbrella that separates us from the rest of the city. Not this summer though. In a week or two there won't be a leaf in sight. It's a terrible thing. They say they don't want to spray because of the birds, but it would be fine with me if they could make the starlings and grackles drop right out of the sky. Dr. McMillan next door would not agree, or at least he would stop himself from saying such a thing out loud. Doctors must treat everyone alike. It's their job.

Edward was proud of living on this street. He used to write home to his relatives in Ontario and tell them he lived only three blocks from the premier of the province, that the Queen of England drove up our street, waving from an open car. After Edward died, so long ago now, I assumed that same pride. People with good names live here, names like Johnson, Stewart, Ross. People with good names make good neighbours.

For a brief while, after old Mr. Murphy next door died, a young woman with a German shepherd dog rented his house. She had very black hair and was not forthcoming with her last name. "What is your nationality?" I asked her. "Swedish," she said, of all things. "You look a little dark to be Swedish," I told her, "I was not born yesterday." Luckily, the house was sold to a young married couple named Gardner and the "Swedish" girl and her dog were forced to vacate. The Gardners have turned out to be delightful neighbours, although we keep a respectful distance.

Dr. McMillan is the neighbour I rely on. He is wonderful about mowing my grass in summer and keeping the snow off my walk in winter. Not everyone is lucky enough to have a neighbour like that. Laura is absolutely wild about him, always has been. I can see her in his yard now, her blond hair flashing past the spaces between the boards of the fence. She often plays there. She has every right, of course, although Mrs. McMillan doesn't know that.

Dr. McMillan paints the fence every year, first my side, then his. He hasn't always been that particular, didn't have time before he retired. I used to see him leaving the house at all hours of the night, coming home worn out at six o'clock in the morning. My heart would ache for him. People have no respect for the private lives of doctors. I know. I've watched him all these years. Working to the point of exhaustion, and her not able to lift a finger to help him out. If only, I used to think. If only it could be me, I would take some of the weight off his shoulders.

I saw their wedding pictures once. I had gone to get Dr. McMillan for Edward, and Mrs. McMillan invited me in to wait for him. The pictures were on the fireplace mantel, you couldn't help but notice them.

She was in a wheel chair even then. I don't know what happened; Dr. McMillan never talks to me about her. Not that I expect him to, some things are better left alone. In the wedding picture I could see that she was pretty. But the smile was artificial, just like it is now. Putting up a good front, I suppose. How could anyone be truly happy with legs all crippled up like that? It would be like living in a bubble, I think. Like one of those poor children who can never come out into the real world.

I've often wondered if she knew then that he would never love her. I can understand what happened. He married her, I believe, for the same reason doctors never turn down a patient. In the wedding picture, they are in front of a huge cake covered with decorations. Dr. McMillan is bending down to clasp her hand while she holds the knife. She is smiling, a smile that I know is artificial, a smile that holds him to her like a chain holds a dog. It's a joke, because he's the kind of dog that would never run away.

It's tea time and I'm out of milk. I would like to call Laura home and have her walk with me to the corner store. But the worms are hanging from the trees on threads, dangling like ticker tape all the way down to the sidewalk. When you walk, the threads catch in your hair and the worms cling to your clothing, crawling around your shirt collar and under your sleeve cuffs. They make you feel as if you're already dead, as if you're just another corpse without a name on the way to the undertaker's. I cannot walk down the street with those worms out there. And it's too late in the afternoon to call the grocery store with an order for delivery. Laura will have to drink orange juice and I will have to drink my tea without milk until tomorrow. Luckily, Dr. McMillan drinks his black. I am expecting him tonight for our weekly game of cribbage.

On Thursday nights I'm like a school girl, so nervous I can hardly get the things laid out. When I was young, when Edward was still alive and Dr. McMillan was just establishing his practice, I thought it would be wonderful to be grown out of such foolishness, such painful foolishness. Now that the pain is gone, I'm thankful I still have the girl inside me. Perhaps it's what keeps him coming. Perhaps he remembers me the way I was. You see, it was painful for both of us.

Before he retired, I was often disappointed. I would get out the cribbage board, just like Edward used to, set it up on the marble coffee table and wait. Then I would see him leave the house with his black bag. I would peek through the front window and wait for him to catch my eye. I'm sorry, that meant. I have to make a call, someone needs me. Now he never misses a Thursday. I suppose his wife thinks he's at his club.

It is quarter to eight. I'm a bit early tonight; he never comes before eight. The cards are on the table next to the board, the tea is in the kitchen under the silk tea cozy. The tray is ready with fine bone china cups and the silver cream and sugar set. I love to get the tea things ready, just as I love to polish the silver on a Saturday afternoon. All of my tea things are good, as are the woodwork and the furnishings in my house. Edward did things that way, always the best. I suppose in some ways I'm fortunate to have married Edward. Really, he married beneath him.

Laura is not asleep. I can see her blond hair through the railing on the staircase. She is on the landing. I march to the bottom of the staircase and motion with my arm for her to get upstairs. She disappears, as children do, but I can still see a few strands of hair trailing from around the corner where the staircase turns to go up the last few steps.

"All right," I say, placing my hands on my hips with authority. "I am going to close my eyes and count to ten. When I open them, I do not want to see you. Not one single strand of hair. I want you in your bed, and if you are not, there will be no ice cream for lunch tomorrow."

I close my eyes. When I open them, the blond hair is gone and I know that she's in bed and will not get up again. I smile to think of her snuggled up under the patchwork quilt, and retire to my chair in the living room. I pick up my novel, my tattered copy of *Jane Eyre*, which I am reading for the hundredth time. I'm too nervous to read now, but when he comes, I will lay the book on the arm of the chair so he will not think I was too anxiously waiting for him. It does not pay to be too anxious.

There is another chair in the living room, one that nobody sits in. It belonged to Edward. He's been gone a long time, but I remember how he would roar if anyone so much as made a move toward the chair. Dr. McMillan sat in it once. It may have been the first time he was ever in our house. Yes, I think it was. He had just moved in next door, newly married, terribly handsome. His office was in his house then. Of course Edward wanted to know all about him, so he sent me to get him to come and look at his in-grown toenail. Dr. McMillan wanted him to come to his office, but Edward would have none of that.

"What's a doctor for if he doesn't make house calls?" Edward bellowed at me. He sent me back again. I remember Dr. McMillan staring at me, standing in his front porch. What could he have thought of this frightened woman from next door?

"You must come," I said. "He's in terrible pain."

He came. And he kept coming too, whenever Edward had some little thing wrong with him.

The truth is, Edward was terrified of disease. He was willing to pay for his own personal physician to be at his beck and call, to rescue him from blood poisoning, staph infection, rare viruses brought into the house on fresh fruit and vegetables. He was terrified and he paid Dr. McMillan handsomely. Edward was lucky enough to have inherited money. And Dr. McMillan needed money. He was fresh out of medical school, struggling to establish a practice in a good neighbourhood.

I was watching that day, the day he sat in Edward's chair. I was in the kitchen baking cinnamon buns and I could not stop

124

myself from glancing up every few minutes to stare at him through the open doorway. I had watched him from our bedroom window, had already fallen in love with him. He could not possibly love her, I thought. He was like Jane Eyre's Rochester, married to a responsibility. Well, marriage isn't always for love anyway. It would be naive to think such a thing.

He knocks so quietly I can hardly hear it. His knock reminds me of Laura's hair, so soft, like the brush of a bird's wing. I open the door and he's there. We don't say hello, just smile at each other, and he steps inside.

We sit on the loveseat in front of the fireplace. The marble coffee table is in front of us, my book lying comfortably on the arm of my chair. He comments, of course.

"And what are you reading now?" he asks, shaking his head. "How you love those old novels. You should have been an English teacher."

"Oh no," I say. "I don't want to have been anything other than what I am. I am quite happy with my life. I wouldn't change a thing." I pause. "Well, perhaps I would change just one thing."

He knows what I mean. He places his hand over mine. I do not look at him, but I know if I do I will see pain in his face.

Dr. McMillan wins our first game. This is not the way things always go. I pride myself on my cribbage game. I sometimes think what a team we would be if we could invite another couple for a foursome. Or if we could go to his club together an afternoon or two during the week. I can't imagine his wife playing cards. They are not the team that we could be.

I do see them out for a walk sometimes, him pushing the wheel chair. He puts up a good front, looks happy enough for the neighbours. Sometimes I see them in the back yard, sitting under a yellow garden umbrella. They have people over occasionally for a barbeque dinner, prepared by Dr. McMillan, and I hear his wonderful warm laugh in the summer air.

I have forgiven him. I cannot forgive Edward.

"Would you like your tea now?" I ask. We usually drink tea as we play. We go through at least a pot, sometimes two.

"Yes," he says, and I slip to the kitchen for the tray.

On the way back I notice a worm on the rim of one of the cups, lifting its horrible body and sliding forward along the fine china lip. I scream, and the tray drops from my hands and crashes on the hardwood floor, missing the Indian rug by inches. Dr. McMillan runs to see what's happened, and I'm on the verge of hysteria, looking at the pieces of china from Edward's collection.

"It's not a catastrophe," he says, taking charge. He gets a roll of paper towels from the kitchen and has the mess cleaned up in no time.

"Come and sit," he says, leading me to the loveseat. "We don't need tea tonight. We'll just visit. We'll just sit here and you won't waste another thought on one or two broken china cups."

He's right, of course. There are at least four dozen cups in the china cabinet. If I live to be a hundred and ninety I'll never need that many cups.

"What do you think about the worms?" I ask him. "Don't you think the city should do something about them?"

"I don't know what they can do," he says. "It would be very expensive for them to spray every tree in the city."

"I don't care about the whole city," I say. "This is one of the finest streets. They have a responsibility. When the Queen of England comes, she drives down this street."

"You're right, of course," he says. "Perhaps I'll call City Hall tomorrow."

"Yes," I say. "You ought to do that. They'll listen to you. You're a doctor."

He laughs. His wonderful laugh that carries on a summer night, carries under the canopy of leaves and through open windows. Many is the night his laughter has comforted me after the neighbourhood has gone to bed.

Edward did not want children. He insisted upon using "protection" whenever he had his way. It was not that often, not so often I couldn't put up with it. "Just close your eyes and it will be over before you know it," my mother told me before I married Edward. "It will be worth it when you bear children, just see if it isn't."

"Please," I asked Edward. "Just one child. I would take care of everything. A child would not inconvenience you, I promise you it wouldn't." He would not even speak of a child. I can still see him sitting naked on the edge of the bed, rolling that hateful thing onto himself.

I did not love Edward. I loved Dr. McMillan. Once, the only

time Edward ever left me alone overnight, Dr. McMillan loved me back the way a man should love a woman. He came to me in my dark bedroom, Rochester coming to his Jane. I wanted to turn on a light and study his face, trace every line with my finger tips, but he wouldn't let me. "There's comfort for us in the dark," he said. "Leave things as they are."

It was a terrible mistake for a doctor to make. I don't know how it could have happened. Edward noticed one night when he saw me in my nightgown. He made me take it off and stand in front of him naked. I feigned innocence, pretended I hadn't noticed the tell-tale workings of my body, pretended I hadn't noticed the slight change in my shape. I stood shivering.

"I'm going next door," he yelled. "It better not be too late to get rid of the goddamned thing."

"He won't do it," I shouted. I had never shouted at Edward before. "He is a doctor. He will not do such a thing."

"He owes me," Edward shouted back. "I set him up. He owes me the shirt on his back. He will do whatever I tell him to."

He went and came back with Dr. McMillan. They talked downstairs, and then I heard their footsteps.

"Leave me alone with her," I heard him say, and he came into my room, closing the door behind him.

We will make arrangements, I thought. Where we will go. When. Edward will take care of her, I would tell him. He has lots of money, you don't have to worry. But I didn't get a chance.

"I'm sorry," he said.

"For what?" I asked. "Don't be sorry."

"I have to do it," he said. "It's the only way."

"Do what?" I asked.

"What Edward wants. I have to do what Edward wants. I'm going to put you to sleep now."

I cried.

"Don't cry," he said. "It will be over with before you know it."

"Don't you want this baby?" I whimpered. "Don't you want this baby either?"

Edward came into the room.

"It's all right," Dr. McMillan said to him. "She's upset. It's understandable."

That's all I remember. Dr. McMillan was a good doctor. In a few days things were as they had been before. As they would remain.

127

THE WEDNESDAY FLOWER MAN

I was fifty-seven years old when Edward died, and when Dr. McMillan paid his respects at the funeral I said to him, "Do come over on Thursday night. I play cribbage at least as well as Edward did."

He smiled, very faintly. His wife was with him, so he was holding back, being cautious. "I'm sure you do," he said.

His wife took my hand then, quite unexpectedly. I froze, not wanting to touch her, unable to pull away. He does not love you, was what I wanted to say to her. He loves me. Me. But of course I couldn't say that.

"Until Thursday then," I said to Dr. McMillan and graciously withdrew my hand.

After he's gone, I look in on Laura. Sure enough she is asleep, curled up like a sack of potatoes under the covers. A few strands of blond hair trail from beneath the quilt and down the side of the bed. How I wish I could bring him up to this room again, show her to him, stand with him.

She will have this house someday, when she is grown up. Dr. McMillan and I will have passed on by then. And there will be no doctor's son next door. His wife, of course, was barren. It's hard to say who will buy his house. Almost anyone can buy a house in a good neighbourhood now, money or no money. And the city is not helping, letting things go downhill, not caring if the worms eat every leaf and leave the trees naked. The Queen of England will drive down this street and they will have to roll up the windows of her limousine.

"This used to be a good neighbourhood," someone will say to her. "It's sad the way things change."

"Yes indeed," she will say, "very sad." Her voice will be soft, dignified, just right for a lady like the Queen.

I can still see her, after all these years, waving from that open car. Edward and I sat in wicker chairs and watched her from our front lawn.

COME DAYLIGHT

Curtis Gates lay in his hospital bed in Swift Current and thought about Muriel and Aaron and Missy and a whole lot of other things he'd tried not to think about for a long time. This heart attack business was doing it to him. He'd had a good look at death, and he had a feeling it was still hanging around somewhere close by. The doctor told him if he didn't quit smoking he shouldn't bother thinking about next year's Christmas presents. It had scared him, he had to admit. But he sure as hell wasn't going to quit smoking. That doctor had another think coming if he thought he could tell Curtis Gates what to do. He'd had a heart attack, sure, but he wasn't going to turn into a goddamned pansy over it.

The sun was shining through the open window. Just a couple more days of this, Curtis figured, and the Poole kid could get to work on the seeding. He hoped the kid would turn out to be a better worker than his old man. Curtis had never hired anybody to do the seeding before, let alone a sixteen year old kid. Well, he was lucky he could get anybody at all. This damned heart attack hadn't given much advance notice.

The Poole kid had been in to see him a couple of days before and Curtis gave him a whole page full of orders, made him write everything down. He was pretty hard on him, made damned sure the kid got the impression Curtis didn't think he could do the job. That would make him work harder, give him something to prove. And if he hadn't proved it by the time Curtis got home from the hospital, he'd fire him faster than it would take the kid to get down off the tractor. He'd finish the job himself, heart attack or no heart attack.

It had been a while since Curtis thought about not having

129

a son, but this business with the Poole kid got him started on it again. If he had a son he wouldn't be lying here worrying about somebody else's boy doing his farming for him. He'd had two but they were both dead. Jeremy Roy had been born with the umbilical cord around his neck and Curtis Junior was killed in a car wreck when he was fourteen. Now there was just Missy and what a headache she'd turned out to be. Hell, he thought, headache nothing. Heartbreak was what she'd turned out to be, nothing short of heartbreak. He should've known from the day Muriel brought her home from the hospital. He'd never heard a baby cry so loud. Missy screamed for a week straight, never slept a wink. Curtis Junior didn't do that. "Must be something wrong with her," Curtis told Muriel. "It's not normal for a baby to cry like that."

Missy wore Muriel right out. Curtis was sure it was Missy that did it. Muriel lost all interest in him, didn't want him touching her anymore, even moved into the spare bedroom. So she could get a better rest, she said. Just for a month or so. The doctor said she needed extra rest. Well, that spare bedroom became Muriel's own bedroom. They hadn't shared a bed in twenty-one years. Except that one time.

Five years ago, it was. The night Missy phoned to say she had moved in with Aaron Christianson. Aaron Christianson, for Christ's sake. A man pushing sixty-five. Muriel had come to Curtis, tried to hold him, but he turned away from her. What made her think he wanted comfort anyway? Hell, what he really wanted was to drive out to Aaron's place and shoot the both of them with the 30.06. That's what his father would have done. Curtis wished the old man was still alive because he really would have done it, to hell with the consequences. He'd kind of favoured Missy too, and got after Curtis a few times for being too hard on her. Like the night Missy came home drunk at four o'clock in the morning with a whole carload of boys, not another girl in the lot. They sat outside in the car and Curtis could hear Missy giggling and laughing, brazen as a cheap whore. Curtis had stormed out in his shorts, thrown open the car door and pulled her out by the hair. He slapped her right there in front of them. "We weren't doing nothing, Mr. Gates," one of them had the nerve to say. So Curtis pulled him out of the car and slapped him too. Then Muriel and the old man came out of the house and when the old man saw what was going on he drew up a fist and laid a good one on Curtis' jaw. Seventy-eight years old he was, and he just about snapped Curtis' head off. The old man favoured Missy all right, there was no doubt about that, but if he knew she was laid up with Aaron Christianson he'd be over there with a gun before you could say your mother's name.

Five years ago. After Curtis turned away from Muriel that night he kept wanting to reach over and touch her, see if her skin still felt like it used to, but he was too damned mad at her for moving into the spare bedroom. He couldn't sleep because she was there beside him, and all night he'd had to fight with himself to keep from reaching out. In the morning Muriel got up and made breakfast without saying a word to him. The next night she went to bed in her own room again.

Five years. He hadn't thought this thing with Missy and Aaron would go on that long. It was revenge, he figured. Aaron's revenge because Muriel had married Curtis, and Missy's because Curtis had wanted her to be a boy. And God damn it, they'd had him by the balls the whole time. They'd got their revenge fifty times over. He hadn't played a game of pool in five years, hadn't had a single beer at the hotel, hadn't even gone to church, for Christ's sake. He was like a weak old animal, scared to go out because he was too old for a challenge. If he'd been younger he would have faced up to it. Instead he drank beer at home and left it up to Muriel to get the mail and the groceries. He stopped going to town altogether, started doing his farm business in Swift Current where nobody knew him.

Sons, Curtis thought. If Missy had been a boy this never would have happened. He and Muriel would still be sleeping in the same bed. He and Aaron would still be playing pool and drinking beer on Saturday nights, maybe slipping across the border for a dozen cans of American, Coors or Budweiser. When he and Aaron were younger they used to head across the border once in a while for the weekend. They were too old for that now, had been for a long time, but he missed the trips south for the beer. And it was all Missy's fault. Things would have been a damned sight different if she'd been a boy. Curtis was willing to bet his life on that. What there was left of it. God damn Missy, he thought. God damn her and Aaron Christianson both.

He pulled the white hospital bedspread up to his chin and closed his eyes. All this thinking was making him tired. He was just nicely settled when he heard someone at his door. He opened his eyes. It was Muriel. He should have seen her pull into the parking lot outside his window but he'd missed her because he was too busy thinking. She was wearing her blue spring coat and she had a bunch of flowers in her arms. She'd gone downstairs to the gift shop and bought flowers the first day he was in, like she thought a hospital room wasn't a hospital room without them. Now, before she even took off her coat, she was throwing the old ones in the garbage and arranging the new ones on the stand beside his bed.

"I see you're awake," she said finally.

"I swear to God those flowers make me sneeze," Curtis said. "I've been sneezing something awful and I can't think what else could be doing it."

"I wish you hadn't been so stubborn about the hospital at home," Muriel said, taking off the blue wool coat. "It's a long drive to come all the way to Swift Current. You know how I am about driving on the blacktop. Everyone goes so darn fast. I'm just thankful it's late enough in the spring I don't have to worry about ice."

"I did my best," Curtis said. "My heart was trying to stop all winter but I held off until the roads cleared up."

"Don't start in," Muriel said. "I wasn't complaining. Just making a comment, that's all."

Curtis watched her hang the coat on the rack in the corner. When's she going to get a new coat, he wondered. He couldn't remember her wearing any dress-up coat but that one. She might even have been wearing it when they got married. But it couldn't be that old. She must have bought the same coat over and over again. Women did that, didn't they? Unless they were Mila Mulroney or Princess Diana or someone like that.

"I brought you a book," Muriel said, taking a paperback out of her bag. "The *Guinness Book of World Records*. I thought you might find it entertaining."

The *Guinness Book of World Records*. Jesus, what next? Why would he want to read about people doing stupid things like eating school buses or standing on their heads for days at a time?

Muriel seemed to know what he was thinking and laid the book on the table by his bed. Curtis closed his eyes again and pretended to go to sleep. It didn't matter whether his eyes were open or not. Muriel would have picked up a magazine to read.

She knew as well as he did they didn't have enough to say to keep them busy for a whole afternoon.

It was his stubbornness that worried her. She'd never met such a stubborn man in her whole life. She had no idea what would happen later this afternoon. She didn't know if Aaron would be with Missy or if Missy would come alone. Either way, something was bound to happen because Curtis was so stubborn, and Muriel was glad this was going to take place in a hospital, close to medical attention for whoever would need it.

He wasn't really sleeping and she knew it. He did this all the time at home. He'd be sitting in the armchair watching TV and would quickly close his eyes when she walked into the room. She'd been letting him get away with it for years, even found it amusing that he didn't know she knew what he was up to. Well, maybe that's what he'd do when Missy got there. Close his eyes and ignore them all. Maybe that was the best Muriel could hope for.

She had lied to Missy.

"He's asking for you," she'd said.

"Aaron too?" Missy had wanted to know.

"No," Muriel had said. She couldn't bring herself to tell that much of a lie. "He didn't say not to ask him, though," she'd added. Missy had sounded so hopeful.

Muriel looked at her watch, then pulled the *Good Housekeeping* magazine out of her purse. She'd stopped at the mall on the outskirts of Swift Current and gone into the bookstore. It was the first time she'd ever driven into the mall's parking lot and she'd been terrified. The traffic was always so bad at the junction and she was afraid she'd panic at the light and forget how to turn left. She was fine driving on country roads, but the city traffic scared her half to death.

Still, she'd turned left into the mall instead of going to the hospital gift shop and she knew why. She did it because it had suddenly hit her that Curtis might die and if he did she would have to know how to make a left-hand turn in the city. She would have to know how to do that and a lot of other things besides. She'd already had to go to the bank and make some arrangements so the Poole boy could get what he needed to do the farming. She hadn't known until she talked to the manager that she could sign cheques. Curtis had always given her cash for everything.

She couldn't read the magazine. Just thinking about such things brought on a terrible fear that he would die soon, maybe even right here in this hospital room. The doctor had told Muriel privately that Curtis would be all right and would probably live a good number of years yet *if* he quit smoking.

"He can't expect me to help him if he's going to smoke two packs a day," the doctor said. "His days are numbered if he keeps that up."

Muriel knew Curtis wasn't going to quit smoking. His stubbornness again. If you were to ask him he'd tell you to bury him with a cigarette sticking out from between his lips. It scared her into making the left-hand turn and it scared her into calling Missy. Muriel would never forgive herself if Curtis died and she hadn't at least attempted to do something. She couldn't really say why she hadn't done anything earlier. She supposed it was because she thought there was all the time in the world, and after Missy was a little older Curtis would just naturally see that she hadn't moved in with Aaron just to spite him. Aaron was an attractive man, not so much in the looks anymore, after all he was the same age as Curtis, but he was kind and gentle. And Missy never was like other girls. It didn't surprise Muriel at all that she didn't want to marry some good-looking cowboy, some young buck from the next town. It didn't surprise her either that she hadn't brought anyone home with her from the city. She loved the country, always had. She loved horses, just like her father, and the chances of finding a horse man in the city were pretty slim. At least that's what Muriel figured. As far as she knew, Missy hadn't had a single boy friend the year and a half she lived in Saskatoon.

Of course there was a six-month period there when they kind of lost contact with her. Missy was going through some funny things with her father then, and she'd chosen to stay away for a while. She'd written a few letters to let them know she was all right, but she'd made it clear she didn't want to see them until she had some things sorted out. As far as Curtis was concerned that was just fuel for the fire, but Muriel understood. It was hard for girls growing up these days. There were so many choices. As long as Missy wasn't taking drugs, Muriel had faith she would be all right. And if she was on drugs, Muriel would have known. She was sure of it. She didn't believe those stories in the magazines about parents with alcoholic children or children addicted to heroin living right under their roof and them not knowing about it. It just wasn't possible. Besides, if Missy had been taking drugs she would have gotten right on the phone and called them up, challenged them with all the details. Missy had always done things like that, from the time she was a little girl. Trying to get attention, Muriel supposed. You'd think she'd have gotten a lot of attention, one little girl with two parents all to herself. But really, she'd had to share them with Jeremy Roy and Curtis Junior. Even though they weren't there. Even though she'd never met them. It would be unrealistic to try to pretend that wasn't true. Curtis had wanted those boys so bad.

Muriel's faith in Missy had nothing to do with believing strange things don't go on in perfectly normal families. Look at her and Curtis. Sleeping in separate bedrooms all these years. She didn't really know how that all came about. It had something to do with Missy. Missy had been such a poor sleeper and Muriel had had to get up several times a night with her. Sometimes every half-hour, all night long. And Curtis was so miserable if he didn't get his sleep. It was hard for him to get up at five-thirty every morning when Muriel and Missy had kept him awake all night.

Yes, it had something to do with Missy and her poor sleeping, but Muriel had to admit it had something to do with Curtis' wanting her too. She was so tired those years when Missy was small. She couldn't bear his hands on her. He was so demanding. He didn't expect her to enjoy it, but he wanted her to respond to him, to want him to want her. And she just was not capable of that, not then. Not with Missy. Not after losing the baby and then Curtis Junior. It was all too tiring, so she had moved her things into the spare room, just until she got her strength back.

And there did come a time when she wasn't so tired anymore, but somehow it was too late. She sensed that Curtis no longer wanted her in his bed. For a while, she suspected he was seeing someone else. Then she decided he was tired out too, and it was easier to leave things as they were. She missed him, though. She missed his touching her, his wanting her. Sometimes she would lie in bed and touch her own body, close her eyes and pretend that her hands were Curtis' hands. Then she would be overwhelmed with shame, and she would put a pillow over her face and pray for morning.

Once, the night Missy phoned to say she was moving in with Aaron, Muriel did go to Curtis. She hadn't wanted comfort. She was sure that's what Curtis thought, that she had gone to him for sympathy. No. She had wanted something else, something they had denied each other. And Curtis turned away from her and she knew that she would never have it again. She had decided to stop thinking about it after that and be thankful for what she had. She and Curtis lived together pretty well, all things considered. Some people had it a lot worse.

Muriel had another little attack of fear about Curtis dying. The white hospital bed took a lot away from him, made him look like he had no colour. She was glad again that she'd called Missy, no matter what happened when she got here.

Muriel had no regrets about marrying Curtis. She would have married him anyway, even if Aaron hadn't signed up and gone to England. Maybe she hadn't told Curtis that. She couldn't remember. She told Aaron, when he came back. She told him everything, felt obligated. She told him openly and honestly that she had married Curtis Gates and had wanted to marry Curtis Gates ever since his father bought the place down the road. Aaron hadn't ever come right out and asked her anyway, so it wasn't as though she had done anything wrong.

Had she really never told Curtis that she was planning to marry him all along? It was hard to believe she'd overlooked that, but she supposed she had. There didn't seem to be any reason to tell Curtis, and personal things like that just made him uncomfortable. Had Aaron ever told Curtis what she'd said? Probably not. In all the time Curtis and Aaron spent together, all those games of pool, all those Saturday nights in the beer parlor in town, Muriel didn't suppose they had ever talked about her. Why would they? Until Curtis got the notion that Aaron took up with Missy just to spite him, and Muriel was pretty sure that was what he figured, there didn't seem to be any reason to even think about it. It was all in the past, a long time ago, when they were young. Different people, really. Missy's Aaron Christianson was a different Aaron Christianson from the one Muriel had known in 1944. At least it seemed like that when she was trying to figure it all out. It was important to Muriel that she get it figured out. Everything made sense, if you could just get it figured out right.

Missy thought Aaron's 1954 Chev pick-up was fun to ride in. He was so proud of that truck. She had talked him into installing a stereo tape deck, and on the way to the hospital in Swift Current they listened to Emmylou Harris and sang along in harmony.

"God damn, she's got a voice," Aaron said.

"She used to sing with this guy named Gram Parsons," Missy said. "I think they were living together, maybe even married. Anyway, he wrote a lot of really good songs. Then he died. Someone found him dead in a hotel room."

"How do you know all this stuff?" Aaron asked. "How in the hell do you find all this stuff out?"

"I just do," Missy said. "She's really nice looking, don't you think?" Missy held up the case for the tape.

"How in the hell can I tell anything from that?" Aaron said. "The picture's the size of a match cover. Can't tell anything from that."

"Well, she is. Take my word for it. And she always wears really nice boots. All rhinestoned up. Nice colours like pink and blue."

"I suppose you want a pair of pink boots with rhinestones?" Aaron asked, grinning.

"Yeah," Missy said. "When we strike oil on the back forty."

"We don't have a back forty."

"Well, whatever we have. You know what I mean."

Aaron was pleased to be making this trip, Missy could tell. She had lied to him, told him that her father was asking for him. He wouldn't have come otherwise. And Missy wanted him there. If her father was prepared to settle with her, he'd better be prepared to settle with Aaron too. That was the only way it would work.

The whole thing was dumb. So Aaron was old. So he was her father's friend. What difference did it make? Her father should have been glad she'd fallen in love with someone he liked. Her mother didn't approve either. Missy hadn't even tried to go home after that first time. Her father had actually stood in the yard with a shotgun or rifle or whatever it was and said he'd shoot them if they stepped out of the truck. It was so stupid. She should have phoned the police, but Aaron said they should just head on home and let Curtis settle things in his own mind.

He was so sensible, Aaron was. He never got mad, never lost his temper. He was the gentlest man she'd ever met. Her mother had more or less said that too, even though she didn't approve, the first time Missy ran into her in town.

"I know he's a good man," Muriel had said. "I just wish you'd gone about this a little differently. It was a shock to your father, you know, coming without warning like that. It's not usual, a young girl and an older man, especially not when you've grown up around him."

That was just it. Missy had had a crush on Aaron Christianson for as long as she could remember. He had been married of course, had teenaged kids even, but Missy didn't care about that. It wasn't serious then. You could have a crush on whoever you wanted to. The only thing that bothered her now was the suspicion there had once been something between Aaron and her mother. Missy didn't know why, but that dated him more than his friendship with her father or his having grown-up kids.

She looked at Aaron driving down the highway and singing along with the tape. He didn't look too old. He still had his own teeth. Quite a few of them were missing, true, and the ones he had left had tobacco stains on them. But he didn't have to take them out at night and soak them in a jar on the counter. And he wasn't bald. He wasn't even grey. Fifty years of wearing a cowboy hat had made a permanent ring around his head, where his hair went flat no matter what, but the top was as thick and dark as Ronald Reagan's.

Missy wondered if Ronald and Nancy still pleased each other in bed. She tried to picture them doing it, then decided they probably didn't. Like her mother and father. Like Aaron and Amanda. Aaron told her once that Amanda hardly ever wanted to do it. Unless she was trying to get pregnant. She would endure him as often as he wanted until the seed was planted, then she would cut him off. God. Missy couldn't imagine what that must have been like.

Although Missy didn't wish anybody dead, she figured Aaron was probably a lot happier with her than he had been with Amanda. And Missy was certainly happier now than she had ever been in her life. A little over five years ago she had been in pretty bad shape. Post-natal depression probably. She didn't know what else could be wrong. Giving up the baby hadn't been

138

that hard, she knew it was best for both of them. It was a bad time, though, and she'd lain in bed at night and wondered why she hadn't just gone home instead of trying to keep it a big secret. Her mother would have taken it all in stride, she knew that. Her father would have ranted and raved and called her every name he could think of, but she supposed he would have eventually settled down and accepted it as one more thing she had done to make his life miserable. Well, that was all in the past now. She'd managed to get through it without them even finding out and except for this rift in the family, things were fine. Better than fine. Really good.

She wasn't too worried about her father and his heart attack. Her mother had assured her he would be right as rain in another couple of weeks. They had his blood pressure stablized with drugs and were trying to get him to quit smoking. If they could just get this stupid thing settled today, once and for all. As mad as she could get at her father because he was bull-headed, she didn't want him to suffer. He'd suffered in his life already, she knew that. She'd heard about the baby and Curtis Junior and how bad he wanted sons. She'd actually thought about Curtis Junior a lot because there were pictures of him and people even said they looked alike. He'd died when he was fourteen. A bunch of kids drunk in a car. The year she'd turned fourteen had been a tough year for her. She kept thinking about Curtis Junior, her brother that she'd never met, being the same age as her and dying. It was creepy. She'd started going to parties and drinking a lot. And when she was drunk in a car on the way home she'd think, "Am I going to make it? Or am I going to die?" And she'd close her eyes and try to imagine what it felt like to die in a car wreck. There were always boys then who knew she was drunk and they'd try things, but she never let them get anywhere. She wasn't interested in them at all. They were too stupid. They just had the booze and the cars.

"I got to stop a few places before I go to the hospital," Aaron said. "How about I drop you off?" They were at the junction by the shopping mall and Missy hadn't even noticed.

"What do you have to get?" Missy asked.

"Just never mind," Aaron said. "You always were too snoopy for your own good."

"I'm kind of scared to go in there alone," Missy said.

The light turned green and they moved forward in the traffic.

"Might be better," Aaron said. "He might want to see you alone for a bit."

Missy remembered the lie about her father wanting to see Aaron at all. "I guess I should go ahead. Drop me off then, but don't be too long."

Aaron reached over and squeezed her thigh.

"Aren't you a bossy little cuss," he said. "I'm an old man. I don't need no young thing telling me what to do." He was grinning.

"Yes you do," Missy said. "You old guys can't look after yourselves properly. Especially you widowers. You're just damned lucky you ran into me in Saskatoon."

"Damned lucky," Aaron said, pulling up in front of the hospital. "Now get out and go face the music."

"Yeah," Missy said, climbing out. "That's what it will be all right." She looked back in the open window. "Don't take too long, okay?"

"I'll be along right smartly," Aaron said. "Hell or high water."

"Good," Missy said, starting up the cement steps. She stopped and stared in the big glass doors at the top. Then she went inside.

Aaron knew what he was looking for but he wasn't sure where to find it. He tried a few department stores like Woolco and the Met, then decided he'd have to go to an electronics place, Radio Shack maybe. He couldn't find a pool game though, so he had to settle for electronic baseball.

"Present for a grandson?" the kid behind the counter asked as he rang it up.

"Hell no," Aaron said. "Present for me. And show me how to work the damned thing before you wrap it up. I never was any good at following those instruction sheets. Especially if they're in German or Japanese."

The kid showed him how to work it and it looked easy enough.

"I suppose I can remember that," Aaron said. "Throw some extra batteries in there too. Don't want to run out in the middle of something big."

Aaron threw the package in the open window of the pick-up and walked down the street to the liquor store. He bought a six-pack of Coors beer, walked back to the truck and headed to the hospital. He looked at the six-pack on the seat beside him. Coors beer wasn't the same now that you could buy it Canada, but the name still had some sentiment attached to it.

COME DAYLIGHT

It was hot. It always seemed hotter in the city. All that pavement and concrete soaking up the heat, then spitting it back out at you. He sat in the hospital parking lot for fifteen minutes fiddling with his new contraption, making sure he knew how to use it. Just in case. Then he wrapped two bottles of beer in his jacket and walked up to the front doors where Missy had disappeared an hour earlier.

When he got to the top step, he sat down. What was he going to be walking in on? He had no idea. He'd known Curtis Gates for most of his life, but he had no idea how he was going to react to this one. If things had gone really badly, Missy would have been waiting for him in front of the hospital. The nurses would have asked her to leave if she'd upset Curtis too much. He'd just had a heart attack. They wouldn't let her stay if he was getting all worked up and raising Cain.

He hoped for Missy that things had gone well. Curtis had been his friend for a long time, but Aaron could get pretty worked up himself thinking about what a bastard Curtis had been sometimes. All because she wasn't a boy. Aaron remembered Curtis saying when Missy was born that girls were nothing but trouble. Can't expect no help out of them, he'd said, just trouble. Curtis was downright mean to her on occasion, and Missy such a sweet little thing. Wild, there was no getting around that, but sweet all the same. And crazy about horses. He'd never seen one so horse crazy. Just like her dad. And the bastard wouldn't buy her a pony for love nor money. Aaron used to put her up on the saddle in front of him and ride her all over the place. When she got older there was no stopping her. She'd just go out and catch whatever horse she wanted, whether Curtis gave her the okay or not.

It had to be tough for her, growing up in the shadow of those two boys. She talked to him about it now sometimes when they were lying in bed at night. They did that a lot. Just lay in bed and listened to her tapes and talked. He'd never talked to anybody in his whole life the way he talked to Missy. Sometimes, in the dark, he'd say to her "What in hell is a young thing like you doing with an old fart like me? Come daylight," he'd say, "you're going to pack your saddlebags and leave." It became a joke between them. Come daylight. She came up with all kinds of things she was going to do to him come daylight, most of them pleasurable. But sometimes he'd wake up just before dawn and he'd ask himself, "What is she doing with me?" Times like that he'd lie there and shake because he was so damned scared she'd ask herself the same question and not be able to come up with an answer good enough to keep her there. But those other times, when they were lying in bed talking, he knew that she needed him as much as he needed her.

For a while, a long time ago, he thought it would be him and Muriel. They started seeing each other while Curtis was off working in the bush in British Columbia. Aaron figured there'd be a big confrontation when Curtis came back, but Curtis acted as if he didn't care. Aaron knew Muriel was having a hard time sorting things out so he signed up and went to England. When he came back Muriel had a long talk with him, seemed to think it was a really big deal, her marrying Curtis instead of him. But it didn't really matter. He wasn't bothered in the least, knew she was sweet on Curtis and always had been. He'd married Amanda a year later and the kids started coming and he didn't think about anything after that but working and eating and sleeping and staying out of Amanda's way. He'd liked the kids, three girls and a boy. The girls were all married and living on farms around the country. His son had gone to veterinary school and lived in Alberta now, had a good practice. All of his kids knew about Missy and none of them had fallen over dead about it. They didn't visit often, but that was all right too.

Aaron had never been able to figure out exactly what it was about Curtis. He had the biggest chip that ever sat on anybody's shoulder and it didn't just grow there after he lost those two boys. It had been there all along. Just got a little bigger as life gave him a few low blows. Aaron supposed it might have had something to do with the old man. He'd been a tough bugger and, now that he thought about it, Curtis was like him.

In lots of ways, Curtis was a good man, but by God Aaron was glad he didn't live in the same house as him. There were times over the years when he thought Muriel must be about the strongest woman on earth to put up with him and not make a single sound about it. He didn't know until Missy told him that they didn't share the same bed, hadn't for years. Curtis had sure never said anything to him about that. But then, it wasn't so unusual. He and Amanda might as well have slept in separate beds. Get rid of the expectation, get a better night's sleep without thinking about wanting something you couldn't have.

Aaron looked at his watch. Jesus. He'd been sitting on the step for half an hour staring at the sky. Missy'd kill him for leaving her on her own all that time. He stood up and grabbed the door handle. He had to stand there for a minute, waiting for the stiff to go out of his knees so he could walk down the hall looking like a visitor and not an inmate.

Curtis was asleep. Aaron sat in a chair beside Missy and took his hat off. He still had the beer wrapped in his jacket and the bag from the electronics store. He put them on the floor under his chair. He said hello to Muriel and she answered him civil enough, though quietly. Missy gave him a funny look, like where have you been, and he winked at her.

It was the stupidest thing, the three of them sitting there staring at Curtis sleeping, not saying anything. There were flowers by the bed, and Aaron felt like he was going to sneeze. He never could stand flowers in the house. Curtis looked the same as ever, a little paler maybe. He had an intravenous needle hooked up to his hand and that didn't do anything for anybody, made you look like you were attached to the hospital bed permanent-like.

Aaron knew Curtis was faking. He figured Missy and Muriel knew it too. It amazed him that the old bugger could make such fools out of them, sick or not. There they all were, just sitting and watching him breathe in the hospital bed, Curtis forcing silence on the room as though it were a church or a funeral parlor. Aaron wondered if Missy had been this quiet since he dropped her off. Hard to imagine, but it looked that way. She'd always seemed so independent. How could Curtis have this effect on her? How could he have this effect on Muriel? She was sitting on her chair like a lady-in-waiting, afraid to say boo. Aaron sat there in the oppressive silence, feeling the sweat run down his sides. Why did they keep hospitals so goddamned hot anyway? They were like giant incubators. Someone should tell the know-it-all doctors there's a far cry between a hen's egg and a grown man.

Muriel's picking up her magazine was the last straw. God damn, Aaron thought, if he was spending the afternoon watching Curtis breathe and Muriel read *Good Housekeeping*. It was obvious that very few, if any, words had been exchanged between Muriel and Missy. And he doubted if Curtis had even had the decency to open his eyes and look at Missy. Aaron didn't care for himself, but he cared for Missy. And Muriel. He cared for her too.

Aaron reached under his chair and pulled out the two bottles of beer. He cracked them both and stood up.

"Curtis," he said, stepping over to the bed. "I know you're just playing possum and Missy and Muriel here know it too. You think you're putting one over on us, but you aren't. You know damn well we're here and you know why too. Now if you don't open up them eyelids I'm going to pour Coors beer all over your stubborn head."

Nothing. Not a flutter. Then he heard Muriel's voice, strong and commanding.

"Don't you dare pour beer on him, Aaron Christianson. You'll make things a whole lot worse than they are already."

Aaron looked at Muriel, surprised by her aggressiveness. Was she protecting Curtis, defending this asinine behaviour? If Missy and Muriel hadn't been in the room Aaron would have said something a whole lot stronger to Curtis, jolted those eyelids open right smartly. Aaron took a swallow of beer from one bottle and put the other down on the table next to the flowers. He reached under his chair for the game and pulled it out of the bag.

"Okay, Gates," he said. "I brought this here gadget with me. Electronic baseball. Made with micro chips and stuff. Tried to get pool but they don't make such a thing. You want to have a game or no?"

He watched the eyelids. Still nothing.

"Just let him be, Aaron." It was Muriel again. He decided to ignore her.

"Coors beer and a good game. Just like the old days. What do you say?"

Nothing. It wasn't working. And Aaron knew he could stand there staring at Curtis' eyelids all day and he wouldn't see those lashes move. Curtis was that damned good at it.

"Okay," he said, throwing the game on the bed. "If that's the way you want it, you stubborn old fool." He took another swallow of beer. He was pissed off. Curtis Gates really pissed him off. Always had. Aaron suddenly realized he had a whole lot of things he wanted to say to him and the heart attack wasn't going to stop him. In fact, the heart attack made it more important to get them said because damned if the lights were going to go out on Curtis with him not knowing just how much he pissed Aaron off.

"You're a son-of-a-bitch, Curtis Gates," he said for starters. "A self-centred son-of-a-bitch."

"Maybe this wasn't such a good idea." That was Missy and she was standing beside him with her hand on his arm, trying to lead him away from the bed.

"It's time these things were said," Aaron told her, refusing to budge. He turned on Curtis again.

"All your life you been bossing people around. Treating Muriel like your housekeeper. Treating Missy like a stray cat Muriel brought home from somewhere."

"Aaron Christianson," Muriel said, beside him now, grabbing his other arm. "If you don't leave right this minute I will never speak to you again as long as I live."

"Come on, Aaron," Missy said. "We're leaving. Right now." She wasn't kidding. Aaron looked at her and damned if he didn't see Curtis in her eyes and her cheekbones and her jaw set like she was going to break all her own teeth if she didn't loosen up. It was the same look Curtis got on his face when he was breaking a horse, an all or nothing kind of look. He felt himself being pulled toward the door and he kept his eye on Curtis to see what would happen. Nothing. Not a goddamned thing.

In the hallway, Missy stopped pulling on him and Muriel dropped his arm and went back into Curtis' room without looking at him.

"I don't need you to stick up for me," Missy said, mad as he'd ever seen her.

"Fine," Aaron said. "And I don't need you to get in between me and a job that needs doing."

Missy didn't seem to have much to say in response to that, so they headed for the parking lot and sat in the truck while Aaron finished his warm beer. He offered some to Missy but she shook her head and sat staring out the window, listening to Emmylou Harris sing. Aaron didn't know whether to be mad or sad that, even with his eyes closed, Curtis could control everything around him.

"Imagine him being that damned good at it," Aaron said as

he dropped the empty beer bottle on the floor and put the key in the ignition.

Curtis was dying to open his eyes. The parking lot was just outside his window and he knew he'd be able to watch them drive off. Maybe he'd be able to watch them fighting; Missy had been mad as hell when they left. Curtis had never known what you were supposed to teach daughters, but he kind of liked the fact she'd picked up his disposition. Muriel said it was stubbornness, but she was wrong. It was just plain standing up for yourself.

He was dying to open his eyes and watch, but Muriel was back in the room. He didn't want her to know he was the least bit interested in Aaron and Missy and how Aaron looked when Missy was mad at him. He could feel the damned game or whatever it was where Aaron had thrown it on the bed and he wanted to knock it off but that would be admitting he knew it was there. He'd just have to wait until Muriel moved it. There was the beer by the bed too. He wondered if it was cold. A cold beer would be good in this suffering hot room. Maybe Muriel would pretend she brought it when he woke up and he'd get to drink it after all. He'd better hurry up if that was going to happen though, because if a nurse came in she'd whisk it away on him as if it were rat poison.

He was just about to stir a little and maybe work up a groan when he felt the game being lifted off the bed. Then he heard Muriel running the water in the bathroom sink. He opened his eyes to check and, sure enough, the beer was gone. God damn it. God damn Muriel. She should have known he'd want it. She could have made something up so he'd get to drink it. She came out of the bathroom and hid the bottle in the inside pocket of her blue coat.

He quickly shut his eyes again and decided to feign sleep for a while longer. It crossed his mind that he could maybe get into the *Guinness Book of World Records*, not that he'd want to. But today had sure as hell been a challenge. He figured that he'd fooled Aaron all right. Aaron had been suspicious, but Curtis knew his eyelids hadn't fluttered once the whole time Aaron was standing over him giving him a piece of his mind. Curtis had actually wanted to laugh, that had been the hardest part, not laughing.

146

He was having a hard time not laughing all over again when he felt Muriel crawl up on the bed. Jesus, what was she doing? The urge to laugh left him. She settled down beside him, then lay still. Curtis wanted to roll over on his side away from her but he knew he wouldn't be able to because she was lying on top of the covers. A feeling of panic set in, like he was trapped under the covers and couldn't breathe. He felt as if the bed had been made up with him in it, the sheet stretched tight over him and jammed under the mattress. He wanted to thrash, kick wildly, rip the covers out from under Muriel. But he couldn't do that. It would be too obvious.

Whatever she was up to, he'd just have to wait it out. Take a deep breath, Curtis told himself, and concentrate. She couldn't stay there for long, it would be too uncomfortable. Curtis figured she must be perched on the very edge of the bed because she wasn't touching him. How could she do this to him on such a hot day? For once, Curtis wished a nurse would come in to do something to him. She would make Muriel move. They had rules about visitors on the bed, didn't they?

Take a breath and think about something else, Curtis told himself. Sooner or later she'd have to move. She couldn't stay there forever.

DEAD RABBITS

Marra is not having a good time. She's sitting on the beach massaging her white stomach, wondering where the pain is coming from. Maybe she has an ulcer or a tumour. Maybe she shouldn't have come here. She had needed to get away for a while and one of the other research assistants at the university suggested this spot, a northern fishing resort. Plenty of hiking trails, he'd said. Incredible scenery. Marra had loaded up her Toyota station wagon and headed out. She doesn't own a tent, but the back seat folds down and she sleeps there.

The place is scenic, Marra has no doubts about that. The lake is clear and black, dotted with tiny islands. At night the loons call back and forth across the water, and this morning Marra saw a Great Blue Heron rise from a huge precambrian rock off shore. But she isn't having a good time. There's something eating at her stomach from the inside out. She feels like she's swallowed broken glass and beer bottle caps and hot dog buns infested with maggots.

Marra's been here for a week. Yesterday it rained and she spent the day driving around in her station wagon. There wasn't much to see from the road, just bush and the odd cabin with wood smoke drifting up from the chimney. On the way out of town she passed through the Indian reserve and the poverty appalled her. Some kids were playing a game, taking turns jumping over a dead dog. Marra kept her eyes straight ahead.

Today it's hot. She sits on the beach in her bathing suit and tries to imagine what she'd look like with a sun tan. She had attempted to go swimming earlier, but the water was icy cold and she thought her heart might stop if she tried to submerge herself in it.

149

She has a picnic lunch with her, crackers with peanut butter and banana. As she takes the crackers out of the sandwich bag, some kids run by and kick sand all over her towel. They're chasing an orange kitten that's darting in and out among the people on the beach. The kids are tough kids and Marra knows they'll tell her to fuck off if she butts in. She doesn't say anything to them, but she hopes they don't catch the kitten.

She doesn't feel like eating, but she forces herself to. Maybe peanut butter is good for ulcers. Maybe it coats your stomach like glue and holds everything together. She takes a bite, then chokes it down with warm apple juice.

She notices a group of kids with a baby stroller at the water's edge. They're laughing and pushing it into the water. She wonders where their mother is and expects to hear a voice shouting from a blanket somewhere. It's one of those strollers that fold up like an umbrella; it was probably expensive and Marra knows the kids shouldn't be playing with it in the water.

The kids push it until the wheels and seat are submerged, then Marra hears a wail. She is shocked to realize there's a baby in the stroller. She is outraged. She looks around the beach to see if anyone is minding the kids but no one seems to be. A few people are watching with interest, a few look concerned, but the baby's parents are obviously not there. Marra is just about to go and rescue the baby herself when the kids pull the stroller out of the water. The baby stops crying instantly.

Marra goes back to her peanut butter and crackers and tries not to think. The baby is all right. It won't drown. She watches as the kids try to wheel the stroller away from the water's edge. The wheels won't turn in the sand, and the kids are all pushing hard from behind. The baby is quiet. They make their way slowly toward her towel and as they come closer she notices that the safety strap is not done up around the baby. It's a wonder it hasn't fallen out, the way they've had to push the stroller through the sand. Marra's peanut butter lunch is not helping her stomach and it sits like a ball of raw dough. One of the kids runs across the sand to a blanket where nobody is sitting. He comes back with a baby bottle filled with something purple. It looks like Grape Crush.

The stroller gets stuck in the sand right next to Marra. This is her chance to say something to the kids. But what? Do up the safety strap? Is that going to fix what's wrong here? What's

150

really needed, Marra thinks, is a miracle. Marra looks at the baby, looks right into its eyes. The baby looks back at her and sucks on the plastic bottle with purple stuff in it. The ball in Marra's stomach grows. The baby takes the bottle out of its mouth and smiles at her. *Go and see Our Lady of Lourdes*, the baby says to Marra in a wonderful sugary voice. Then it sticks the bottle back between its lips and sucks noisily.

Marra is driving down the highway trying to remember where she saw the sign saying *Shrine of Our Lady of Lourdes, 7 kilometres*. She had passed it somewhere on her way north; she remembers seeing it and wondering what it was all about. Lourdes, she recalls, is the place in France where a little girl saw the Virgin Mary. She can't remember whether or not the Virgin spoke to the girl, and if so, what she said.

Marra wonders what she'll find at the shrine. A cross painted on a rock? A cairn? A spring with clear cold water, like at Lourdes? If there is a spring there, she will bathe in it, try to wash this lump out of her stomach, cleanse it away. That must be what a shrine is for, conjuring some kind of Catholic magic.

She stays on the same road she took when she came north a week ago. She knows she passed the sign, remembers it clearly now, more clearly with each mile she drives. She stops for gas at a roadside Esso and asks the attendant if he has heard of the shrine. He has not.

She's been on the road now for five hours and still she hasn't seen the sign. She hasn't eaten since yesterday, had no appetite this morning when she packed up her station wagon and left. Not that she had much to pack, a canvas lawn chair, a few dishes, and a bag of charcoal barbeque briquettes. She threw what was left of her food in the garbage. She had to drive through the reserve again on her way out of town, and this time she'd actually closed her eyes for a few seconds.

Marra has driven most of the way back to city and hasn't found the sign. She's positive it isn't this far south. She pulls over onto the shoulder, turns off the motor, and tries to think of where else she might have seen it. The windows of her station wagon are rolled down and she can smell the pavement. She switches on the radio and sits listening to country and western music for a while. She loves country music. Just up the road she can see the body of a dead rabbit, and beyond it two big crows are sitting on a barbed wire fence waiting for her to leave. She's seen a lot of dead rabbits along the highway and supposes this is one of those years when they are particularly plentiful.

As she sits listening to Dwight Yoakam sing *Heartaches by the Number*, she remembers that on the trip north she'd had to turn off the highway for gas. The town had been a few miles in along a gravel road and it's possible she'd seen the sign there. She starts the Toyota, does a U-turn on the highway, and heads back the way she came.

She recognizes the name of the town when she sees it and turns off the highway. Sure enough, at the side of the gravel road is a narrow green sign pointing south. It says *Shrine of Our Lady of Lourdes, 7 kilometres*. Marra considers driving the rest of the way into town for something to eat. It's late afternoon and she should be hungry by now. She isn't though, so she follows the sign's direction and turns south.

The shrine is by the road on the edge of somebody's pasture, a shabby blue building that looks like a small tool shed. It's not at all what Marra had expected a shrine to look like. She gets out and walks around the building. Grass and weeds have grown out of control around it and there's no sign that anyone has been here for years. Marra doesn't know what she expected, plastic flowers maybe, left the way people leave them by grave markers. The blue paint is peeling and some of the shingles have fallen off. A small door near the top of the building looks as if it's supposed to be kept locked, but the latch is unhooked and rusty. Marra reaches up to open the door and the Virgin appears.

Marra has been here now for three days, leaving only once to drive into town for a dozen cans of apple juice. There had been some traffic along the road during the day, but no one seemed to pay any attention to her. She's glad of that, doesn't want to explain to anyone why she's here.

The white plaster face of the Virgin is beautiful. She smiles as though she has it in her power to work miracles. She cradles the Christ child in her arms, and seems to be looking at the baby and out the door of the shelter at the same time. The door has been open now for three days and Marra thinks perhaps the Madonna smiles with pleasure at being able to gaze out upon the prairie. The station wagon is parked so that the Madonna watches over it too. At night, Marra lies in the back with the windows open. The mosquitoes don't bother her. She's preoccupied with the lump in her stomach. She's decided the voice of the baby on the beach was a miracle, and she has not slept since she came here. She's waiting for another miracle.

On the morning of the fifth day it comes. Marra is sitting in the grass staring at the pile of empty apple juice cans when the Virgin speaks to her. Her voice is like that of an enchantress, soft and sweet. Marra recognizes it as the voice of the baby on the beach. *Bury the dead rabbits*, the Virgin says without moving her lips. "What?" Marra asks, jumping up. "What did you say?" But the Virgin does not speak again.

Marra waits all day. She doesn't understand what is being asked of her. Bury the dead rabbits. She must have heard wrong, must have misunderstood. She waits for the Virgin to speak again, to give her some kind of direction, to explain what she wants Marra to do. But nothing comes.

At midnight, Marra decides she has witnessed the miracle and that no more is coming. She must not be greedy. She has heard more than most people. She piles the empty juice cans in the Toyota, kisses the Virgin's painted lips, and closes the door to the shed.

Marra has a shovel with her, a collapsible one from the army surplus store. Up until now she has not used it, and the fact that she has it with her seems to be a part of the miracle. She gently guides the shovel under the rabbit's body and carries it off the pavement to the hole she has dug for it. A hundred yards away, a huge crow dances slowly on the shoulder of the road, lifting one leg then the other, folding and unfolding its black wings. When Marra drives off, it rises into the air and drops down to inspect the bloody stain on the highway. Marra stops and watches in the rear view mirror until the crow spreads its wings again and disappears.

She does what the Madonna told her to do. She drives down the highway, stopping to bury the dead rabbits. She does this all day. When she nears the outskirts of the city, she turns onto a grid road. When that road approaches a town, she turns again. By evening Marra doesn't know where she is, but it doesn't matter because she's doing what the Virgin told her to do. The lump in her stomach seems to be growing smaller and she feels elated.

THE WEDNESDAY FLOWER MAN

The sun is almost down when Marra stops the station wagon for the night. She parks on the shoulder, gets out and crawls under a barbed wire fence into a pasture. She climbs a hill and lies down on the very top, stretching out and molding her body to the earth. She feels the evening breeze on her face, smells the sage and the sweet clover.

Without warning her stomach knots and she is in spasms. She rolls over, comes to her knees and vomits. She vomits again and again, spilling the liquid contents of her stomach onto the top of the hill where it runs downward in rivers. Marra wants to close her eyes so she won't see what's happening to her. But they're wide open as if someone is gripping her eyelids, forcing her to watch. She tries to look up, away from the earth, tries to stop the terrible retching. But it keeps coming and her head is too heavy to lift. She thinks she hears a voice on the wind. "Mother of God," the voice cries. Is it her own voice? Marra doesn't know. When the spasms finally stop, she is too weak to move. She collapses, not caring that she is lying in her own vomit. She lies with her head to one side, her eyes open. She feels as if she has no body.

The moon shines on the pasture. There is a sudden movement at the base of the hill, then all is quiet again. Another movement. Then another and another. Rabbits. The pasture is alive with rabbits. Rabbits with sleek summer fur and bright eyes. Now the baby is there too, laughing, toddling after them on strong, sturdy legs. And the kids that were jumping over the dead dog. And the orange kitten from the beach. All of them playing in the moonlight.

A hawk appears. It circles overhead once, then touches down on top of the hill next to Marra. Together they watch.

MIRACLES NIGHTLY

Things aren't good at Sam and J.J.'s. Sam's been laid off again and just a week ago the doctor told him he has a low sperm count. That was really bad news, because Sam wants more than anything to be a dad.

When J.J. got home from work yesterday afternoon Sam was sitting in front of the TV with a row of empty beer bottles lined up at his feet. "What're you watching?" she asked, suspicious. Sure enough, it was *Nine Lives to Live*.

They've been through this before. Last year Sam was laid off for three months and J.J. just about had to leave him. Not that she was worried he might beat her or anything like that. But he got so bored, and boring, that she could hardly stand to live with him. All he wanted to talk about was *Nine Lives* and what kind of beer he should try next. He became obsessed with finding the absolutely best brand of beer and sat at the supper table making lists of criteria and designing charts for keeping track. And he began spying on the neighbours, counting the sheets on people's clotheslines to see how often they washed them, getting up in the middle of the night to listen for bits of conversation coming through the bedroom window. He even bought a pair of binoculars so he could see right into the living rooms across the street.

"They're for duck hunting," he told J.J., but she knew what he was up to. She came home from work once and found his Lazy Boy recliner pulled right up to the picture window. The drapes were closed except for a three-inch opening, and a row of beer bottles curved halfway around the chair.

"Home so soon?" asked Sam, flapping out of the kitchen in his bedroom slippers, the binoculars around his neck, another beer in his hand. "The moon," he said when he saw J.J. looking at the chair. "You know how you can sometimes see the moon in the daytime. I was just looking for it. Thought I might take up astronomy."

J.J. hit the roof over that, told him he was turning into an old man and he wasn't even thirty yet. She returned the binoculars to the hardware store, moved the Lazy Boy back to its place in front of the TV, and told Sam if she caught him spying on the neighbours again she would call the RCMP and tell them he was a pervert. That night, when she wasn't mad anymore, she tried to turn it into a joke.

"Come on, Sammy," she said, tickling him behind the knees where he's particularly sensitive. "If you say uncle I won't tell anyone you're a preee-vert."

"Stop it J.J.," he said. "Life's got me down. I can't laugh anymore."

Well, that was last year. Now Sam's laid off again and with this extra bad news about his masculinity he's driving J.J. around the bend. He can't decide whether he likes Miller High Life or Molson's Golden better, and thinks he may special order some American brands. He's taken a subscription to *The Guide to Daytime Television*, and J.J. is sick of hearing about Scarlet and Nat and Tanya. In bed at night, when J.J. moves her hands over Sam's body the way she used to, he simply isn't interested.

"I can't do that anymore," he says, pushing her away. "What's the point anyway?"

"Come on, Sammy," J.J. pleads. "How are we going to make babies if we don't do it?"

"Now there's a joke," Sam says. "You heard the man. I'm impotent."

"Jesus," J.J. says. "He said sterile, not impotent. He didn't even really say sterile. He used the word 'unlikely'."

"Unlikely. Sterile. Impotent. What's the difference?" Sam moves over so close to his edge of the bed he might as well sleep on the couch and be done with it.

J.J. lies awake and thinks it's a good thing she has a job or they'd really be in a bad way. She doesn't want to have to move away. She likes this town.

For the most part, it's a lumber town. The men work either in the bush or in the saw mill. But there's a lake two miles down the road, a deep lake with trout in it, and in the summer the tourists come, a lot of fishermen in May and June, and families with tents and camper trailers in July and August. J.J. works at the lake from May through September, cleaning the thirty or so log rental cabins that are scattered along the shore. She and Sylvie do that, and they walk out to the lake together every day.

"It's not a disaster that Sam's laid off," J.J. says to Sylvie. "Not as long as I've got this job anyway. I don't know why things get so bad when he's not working." She doesn't tell Sylvie about Sam's other problem, thinking it would be a kind of betrayal.

"It's his self-esteem," says Sylvie. "Men are like that. Their self-esteem goes right down the tube if they can't be the bread-winner. If I find a man who'll take me and the kids I'll quit work so fast it'll make your head spin."

"You'll find a man," says J.J. She puts her arm around Sylvie and gives her a squeeze. She wants Sylvie to be happy.

They clean the cabins together, taking turns doing the bathrooms. That's the part they hate, imagining some drunken fisherman hunched over, puking his middle-aged guts out. Sometimes it looks like there's been a whole bevy of fishermen in the bathroom, and when it's that bad Sylvie and J.J. clean it together. They're usually finished by about three, and they walk home along the dusty road.

"What's that?" asks Sylvie as they come over the last hill and see the edge of town below them. A tent is what they're looking at, red and white stripes, a circus tent maybe. As they get closer they can read the banner stretched between two metal posts. *The Miracle Tent*, it says in big black letters. Then beneath that: *Cripples Healed, Signs Interpreted, Miracles Nightly, Monday to Friday*.

"Well, there you go," says J.J. "We'll head on in there and you'll find a good-looking man who wants two kids and I'll find a job for Sam and get pregnant."

Sylvie doesn't say anything, seems lost in her thoughts, and when they are beside the tent she stops and stares at it. J.J. stares at Sylvie staring at the tent and suddenly Sylvie seems frail and vulnerable, her blond hair a bit too much like dry grass blowing in an empty lot.

"Sylvie," J.J. says, "just what are you thinking about?"

"Miracles," says Sylvie.

"Well, we aren't going to find any miracles in there," says J.J. "I was only kidding. Don't go funny on me, Sylvie. I couldn't take it if you and Sam went funny on me at the same time."

"To be completely healed," says Sylvie. "That's what I want."

"What are you talking about? You don't need to be healed. There's nothing wrong with you."

"I'm like Sleeping Beauty," says Sylvie. "I need a handsome prince to come along and wake me up."

"Wake you up maybe," J.J. says, "but you don't need to be healed."

When J.J. gets home, she finds Sam in front of the TV. He has taped a 24 x 30 inch beer chart to the wall beside his chair. J.J. sees this as a positive step because it means he's been out to the store for bristol board and felt markers.

"What's new?" she asks, trying to sound cheerful and optimistic.

"Not much," Sam says. "Scarlet just moved in with Benny. Nat has cancer, probably terminal. Tanya's thinking about killing herself but not tonight because she's been invited to dinner on Michael's yacht and he's a really good cook."

"I'm glad your day's been so full," J.J. says.

"Don't bug me," says Sam. "These people are my life. They're all I have."

J.J. thinks maybe she should get Sam another pair of binoculars from the hardware store. At least the neighbours are real people.

After supper she talks Sam into going out. They stop for a beer at the hotel and sit outside. The hotel's fenced-in cement patio is known as the Flamingo Room. Usually the mosquitoes are so bad you can't sit there, but tonight there's a breeze and that keeps them away.

As soon as they sit down, Sam says he can hear church music. J.J. can't, but she remembers the tent and tells Sam about it. She's surprised to notice that he seems interested.

"Miracles nightly," Sam says. "What the hell."

Later, J.J. tries to work her own magic on Sam, but he rolls away from her.

"Not right now," he says. "In a few hours maybe."

J.J. does a crossword puzzle to stay awake, but in a few hours Sam has become nothing more than a warm lump, fused to his side of the bed until morning.

The next day, Sylvie tells J.J. all about what goes on in the miracle tent.

"Beautiful music," Sylvie says. "The kind of music that makes you feel like you're floating about three feet off the ground. And you sing along and you can't believe your voice is making that wonderful sound. I mean, normally I can't carry a tune and I swear I sound like an angel inside that tent. And the voice of the pastor. When he speaks, you're just — lulled. It feels fantastic."

J.J. can't believe what she's hearing. "For God's sake, Sylvie, do you know what you're saying? It's empty-headed. How did you end up in that tent, anyway?"

"I don't know," Sylvie says. "I was out for a walk when I heard the music. I had the kids with me and we all said at once, 'Let's go in there and see what's going on.' It was fantastic. You and Sam should go."

"Not on your life," J.J. says.

Sylvie sings all day at work and it's clear she still can't carry a tune. J.J. recognizes some of the songs in spite of what Sylvie does to them: *We Shall Gather at the River, Onward Christian Soldiers, Amazing Grace.* Somehow *Beautiful Dreamer* gets slipped in and that's when J.J. stuffs her ears with little wads of toilet paper.

"The kids and I are going back tonight," Sylvie says when they reach the tent on the way home. "Do you want to come with us?" The sun shines down on Sylvie's hair and today J.J. is reminded of apricots.

"Not on your life," she says and goes home to Sam who is the very picture of dejection because *Nine Lives to Live* has been pre-empted by news coverage of the Queen Mom's visit to Canada. By the time supper is over with, Sam is in such a depression that J.J. sends him out to walk up the alley.

"Tomorrow's garbage day," she says. "Go see what scandalous items the neighbours are trying to get rid of."

He doesn't come back. At least not until very late that night. And when he does, he is singing at the top of his lungs, drunk with salvation.

"You've been at the tent, haven't you?" J.J. says. "It's a disease, that tent. A cursed disease."

"I was in the alley," says Sam, "and I could hear the music, almost *see* it floating over me like a whole mess of helium balloons. Before I knew it I was in the tent. Sylvie was there. She got her miracle tonight."

"What are you talking about?" J.J. asks. "What kind of miracle did Sylvie get in that tent? All she wants is a man."

J.J. gets to see Sylvie's miracle the next day at work. She brings it with her in her purse, a book on ballroom dancing with charts to show you how to move your feet.

"He figures I need someone more sophisticated than what I'll find around here," Sylvie says. "He figures if I find someone who does this kind of dancing, then I'll have found Mr. Right."

"How much did you have to pay for this miracle?" asks J.J.

"For heaven's sake, J.J.," says Sylvie. "People don't pay for miracles. God, you're suspicious."

Sylvie tells J.J. how the miracles come about. After the singing, the pastor calls for people who want miracles to come to the front. You line up to speak to him and when it's your turn you tell him, right in front of everyone, what kind of miracle you think you need. Then he lays his hands on your head, and tells you what your miracle is.

"And how'd you get your miracle?" asks J.J. "I suppose he pulled it out of the sky."

"I don't know," says Sylvie. "When I got back to my seat it was there, just sitting there waiting for me."

That night J.J. tries to stop Sam from going to the tent, but he's too excited about getting his miracle. When he leaves the house after supper, J.J. follows him. She doesn't go right into the tent, but picks a spot just close enough that she can see what's going on.

The flaps are open. Funny thing though, she can't hear the singing. She can see the pastor with orangey-blond hair up at the front waving his arms around like some famous conductor she's seen on TV. He looks like a goldfish with big white teeth. She can see the choir behind him, eight men and women in white robes swaying back and forth, goldfish mouths opening and closing in unison. Half the town is in there singing and J.J. can't hear a sound, not a single voice.

The singing seems to go on until dark, then the choir sits down and J.J. figures it's time for the handing out of miracles. She slips closer so she can see if Sam lines up, but suddenly the pastor steps down and stomps toward the open tent flaps. He peers out into the dark, almost as though he knows J.J. is out there, then he pulls the flaps shut. Now all J.J. can see is the tent glowing away in the dark, with shadow puppets moving silently inside. She tries to pick out Sam's shadow but can't. They all look the same.

"A tough case," Sam tells her when he crawls into bed at one o'clock in the morning. "Toughest one he's ever had. I have to go back again tomorrow."

"I suppose he's going to pull a job out of a hat for you," says J.J.

"Maybe," says Sam and is asleep before J.J. can even think about working on his other problem. Not that she wants to tonight. She feels like that orange-haired pastor is in bed with them. She thinks she can see his white teeth sparkling away in the dark.

What happens with Sam's miracle is not the way it happens most of the time. The pastor can't seem to conjure up Sam's miracle right there in the tent, so he has to order it special from some kind of mail order catalogue. Sam has no idea what it's going to be, but oddly enough, he gets called back to work the week after the tent has been packed up and hauled off to some other town. Sam hauls all the empty beer bottles to the garage and cancels his subscription to *The Guide to Daytime Television*. That's miracle enough for J.J., but Sam figures there's more coming.

"Jesus," J.J. says. "Do you mean to tell me you stood up there and told half the town you have a low sperm count?"

He doesn't answer, but it looks like that's what he did all right.

Over the next few weeks both Sylvie and Sam drive J.J. crazy. She wishes she'd burned the miracle tent down the first time she laid eyes on it. Sylvie wants her to practise ballroom dancing with her every day after work. J.J. tells her to dance with a broom instead but Sylvie insists a broom isn't the same as a real person. Sam phones from the bush on the radio phone every day to ask if there's anything in the mail. J.J. hates talking on the radio phone because you have to say "over" after everything and that seems particularly silly when you're talking about miracles coming in the mail. Sam still thinks he's impotent and J.J. figures she's going to have to make another appointment with the doctor so he can explain to Sam in medical terms the difference between impotence and sterility. He doesn't want to listen to J.J.'s explanation. He's just waiting for that package.

Come September, it still hasn't arrived. Things are working out for Sylvie though. She's been taking the bus into the city every Tuesday night to go dancing at the Imperial Club and now she has a boyfriend who drives out to pick her up. He seems to like the kids.

"Okay," J.J. finally says to Sam. "Face it. There's no package. It's not coming. Now let's get this stupid problem of yours straightened out. I don't care if we can't have babies. We can adopt. We can get a dog."

But Sam isn't listening. The woman from the post office is at the door with a package in a plain brown wrapper.

"I don't usually make deliveries," she says, "but I know you've been waiting for this." She winks.

As soon as she's gone, Sam rips the paper off.

"What is this?" he asks, staring at the box, blushing like a house on fire. And before J.J. can get a look, he whips it into the bedroom and into his dresser drawer.

"Come on, Sam," J.J. says, following him. "Don't be ridiculous. Show me what it is. I've had to listen to you all this time. I think I have a right to know what it is."

But Sam won't show her, and he is deeply disturbed. Late in the night and on into the morning hours he lies awake in bed, sighing, his back to J.J. He won't go to work in the morning, is still in bed when J.J. leaves to walk out to the lake, is still in bed when she gets home again at three o'clock. When he refuses to get up for supper, J.J. crawls into bed with him.

"Okay Sammy," she says. "You have to tell me what's wrong. If you don't, I'll call your mother."

"It's no laughing matter," he says. "It's embarrassing."

J.J. can see just the back of his head because he's facing the wall and has the covers pulled up to his chin. She reaches out and plays with the cowlick that always sticks straight up from the crown of his head, twists it in her fingers, curls it into a little ringlet.

"Sammy, Sammy, Sammy," she murmurs softly and moves over, snuggles up against his back. "Tell me what's in that package, Sammy." She nibbles on his ear, caresses his ear lobe lightly with her teeth.

"I can't," says Sam. "I want to, but I can't."

"Of course you can," says J.J., searching for his bare toes with her own. "Just start talking and see what happens."

Sam reaches out from under the bedclothes and points to his dresser.

"Have a look," he says. "Have a good look and then start laughing." He rolls over onto his back. "Laugh your head off. See if I care. Laugh your head off while you're thinking 'Jesus, how can Sam be so dumb? How can a grown up adult man be so dumb even if he is impotent or sterile or whatever he is?' "

J.J. slides out of bed and pulls the box out of Sam's dresser drawer.

"I am so dumb," Sam says, "that somebody should shoot me and put me out of my misery."

Body Paints for Lovers," J.J. reads on the box.

"Christ, if I'd have known I was going to grow up to be this dumb I just wouldn't have bothered. I would have refused to be born."

Body Paints for Lovers," J.J. reads again. "I didn't know Holy Rollers were into this stuff."

Sam stares at her. "Nobody is into that stuff, J.J.," he says. "Nobody but whackos, sex perverts, maybe rock star weirdos. I mean, just look at the picture on the front."

J.J. looks at the picture on the front.

"A man and a woman kissing," she says.

"Don't give me that," says Sam, sitting up and grabbing the box. "Look at them. They're naked. They're yellow and blue stripes, for God's sake. On their backs too. Now you can't tell me they painted their own backs. They painted each other, that's what's happened."

"You really are dumb," says J.J. "How can I have been married to you for this long and not known you're so dumb? Of course they painted each other. That's the idea. Want to try it?"

Sam puts his hands over his ears, but J.J. pulls them away.

"Come on, Sammy. Tell me what you want to be. Tell me and I'll paint you up." She is already tearing the cellophane wrapper off, opening the box. "Anything at all," she says. "A train. A grain elevator. A Christmas tree."

Sam doesn't say anything, but he appears to be thinking.

"A dinosaur. An astronaut. A Rhesus monkey." J.J. takes the paints out of the box, six bottles of brilliant colour, and lines them up on the dresser. "A mad dog. An Englishman. A Coors beer can."

"Sperm," says Sam.

"Sperm, you say," says J.J.

163

"Yeah," says Sam. "Sperm. You know. One of those little wriggling things that I don't have enough of."

"Ah," says J.J. "Sperm. I see." She sits on the edge of the bed and thinks about spermatazoa. "It's not everything, you know Sam," she says. "Sperm is not everything."

"I don't care," says Sam. "You asked me what I wanted to be and that's it."

"Okay," says J.J. "Sperm it is."

She dips her fingers in the jars and paints. Head to toe, she transforms Sam into a live, wriggling sperm, pale blue with little red dots on his belly.

"These are your genes," she says. "How many do you want?"

"I don't know," says Sam. "How many's normal?"

"Beats me. How about a hundred and forty-four?"

"Fine."

That's how many he gets. And when J.J.'s done, Sam wants to do a little painting himself. He paints a blue dot on J.J.'s belly, so small you can hardly see it.

"The egg," he says to her. "Can't get anywhere without one of those."

"One more thing," says J.J. She grabs the jar of red paint and stands on the bed. Reaching up, she paints half a dozen red stripes on the ceiling.

"The miracle tent, of course," she says, switching off the light.

Some kind of miracle does happen for Sam and J.J., under the red stripes. And the rest is history.

The THUNDER CREEK CO-OP is a production co-operative registered with the Saskatchewan Department of Co-operatives and Co-operative Development. It was formed to publish poetry, prose, songs, and plays.

Publications

A Sudden Radiance, the first release of the Carlyle King Series. An important anthology of Saskatchewan poetry edited by Lorna Crozier and Gary Hyland. $14.95 pb./$21.95 hc.

The Wednesday Flower Man, fourth in the McCourt Fiction Series. A tough and whimsical collection of short stories by Regina writer Dianne Warren. $8.95 pb./$16.95 hc.

What Holds Up the Moon? A rhyming storybook in full colour for children aged 3 to 8; written by Lois Simmie and illustrated by Anne Simmie. $6.95 pb./ $13.95 hc.

The Fire Garden, fifth in the Wood Mountain Series. New poetry that affirms the spirit against the fires that threaten the earth, by Paul Wilson. $7.00 pb./ $15.00 hc.

Herstory 1988. A practical and informative calendar featuring Canadian women. $8.95 coil-bound.

The Valley of Flowers: A Story of a T.B. Sanatorium. A novel about a young woman whose youth was spent fighting illness, by Veronica Eddy Brock. $4.95 pb.

White Lions in the Afternoon. Poems, drawings, etchings and paintings by Saskatoon writer and artist Elyse Yates St. George. $7.00 pb./$15.00 hc.

Some of Eve's Daughters, third in the McCourt Fiction Series. Compelling stories by a striking new voice, Connie Gault. $8.95 pb./$16.95 hc.

The Old Dance: Love stories of one kind or another. Thirty short stories which examine love, edited by Bonnie Burnard. $4.95 pb.

Heading Out: The New Saskatchewan Poets. A sparkling anthology of poetry edited by Don Kerr and Anne Szumigalski. $9.95 pb./$15.95 hc.

Shaking the Dreamland Tree, number four in the Wood Mountain Series. A strong first collection of poetry offering evocative images of a harsh reality, by Nadine McInnis. $7.00 pb.

Standing on Our Own Two Feet, third in the Wood Mountain Series. Poetry of everyday experiences by William B. Robertson. $7.00 pb./$15.00 hc.

Changes of State. Powerful, arresting poetry by internationally-acclaimed poet Gary Geddes. $7.00 pb./$15.00 hc.

What We Bring Home, the second book in the Wood Mountain Series. Well-crafted poetry by Judith Krause. $7.00 pb./$15.00 hc.

Voices & Visions: Interviews with Saskatchewan Writers. By Doris Hillis. $11.95 pb./$17.95 hc.

Queen of the Headaches. Short stories nominated for the 1985 Governor General's Literary Award, by Sharon Butala. $5.95 pb.

Monster Cheese. A fast-paced, illustrated children's story by Steve Wolfson, for ages 3-8. $5.95 pb./$11.95 hc.

Prairie Jungle. An anthology of songs, poetry, and stories for children ages 6-12, edited by Wenda McArthur and Geoffrey Ursell. $7.95 pb.

Hold the Rain in Your Hands. A definitive collection of the best from five earlier books plus new poems, by Glen Sorestad. $8.95 pb./$15.95 hc.

Territories. Fresh, distinctive poetry by Elizabeth Allen. $6.00 pb.

Double Visions, the first release in the Wood Mountain Series. Poetry by Thelma Poirier and Jean Hillabold. $6.00 pb./$14.00 hc.

Ken Mitchell Country. The best of Ken Mitchell. $4.95 pb.

More Saskatchewan Gold. Exciting, imaginative, masterful short stories by Saskatchewan writers, edited by Geoffrey Ursell. $4.95 pb.

Foreigners. A lively, passionate novel by Barbara Sapergia. $4.95 pb.

Street of Dreams. Poems that recover our lost experiences, our forgotten dreams, by Gary Hyland. $7.00 pb./$15.00 hc.

Fish-Hooks, the second release in the McCourt Fiction Series. Thirteen stories by an exciting new talent, Reg Silvester. $6.00 pb./$14.00 hc.

100% Cracked Wheat. An excellent source of dietary laughter from Saskatchewan writers; edited by Robert Currie, Gary Hyland, and Jim McLean. $4.95 pb.

The Weather. Vibrant, marvellous poems by Lorna Crozier. $6.00 pb.

The Blue Pools of Paradise. A document of secrets, poems by Mick Burrs. $6.00 pb.

Going Places. Poems that take you on a vacation with Don Kerr. $6.00 pb./ $14.00 hc.

Gringo: Poems and Journals from Latin America. By Dennis Gruending. $6.00 pb.

Night Games, the first book in the McCourt Fiction Series. Stories by Robert Currie. $7.00 pb.

The Secret Life of Railroaders. The funniest poems ever to roll down the main line, by Jim McLean. $5.00 pb.

Black Powder: Estevan 1931. A play with music by Rex Deverell and Geoffrey Ursell. $5.00 pb.

Earth Dreams. Startlingly original poems by Jerry Rush. $5.00 pb.

Sinclair Ross: A Reader's Guide. By Ken Mitchell, with two short stories by Sinclair Ross. $7.00 pb.

Odpoems &. Poems by E. F. Dyck. $4.00 pb.

Superwheel, the musical about automobiles. With script by Rex Deverell and music and lyrics by Geoffrey Ursell. $5.00 pb.

All the above may be ordered from your favourite bookstore or from:

coteau books

Thunder Creek Publishing Co-operative
Box 239 Sub #1
Moose Jaw, Saskatchewan
S6H 5V0

McCourt Fiction Series

In the spring of 1983, COTEAU BOOKS announced its *McCourt Fiction Series*, a new venture in high-quality fiction by prairie writers. The series is named in honour of Edward A. McCourt (1907-1972), the distinguished Canadian writer, critic, and teacher.

Ed McCourt's thirteen books of fiction, non-fiction, and criticism are a vital part of the literary culture of Saskatchewan and Canada. They include six fine novels, non-fiction books on Saskatchewan, Canada, and the Yukon and Northwest Territories, a biography, *Remember Butler*, and the pioneering critical work, *The Canadian West in Fiction*.

McCourt's influence as a vibrant and dedicated teacher at the University of Saskatchewan is no less important. He won the respect and love of his students, many of whom became teachers or writers themselves. Wherever they are found, throughout Saskatchewan and Canada, they remember the intellectural excitement of their classes with Ed McCourt.

We at COTEAU BOOKS are pleased to release the fourth book in the *McCourt Fiction Series* — *The Wednesday Flower Man* by Dianne Warren.

About the Author

Photo by Gary Robins

Although this is Dianne Warren's first book, her stories have been widely published. Her work has previously appeared in literary publications including *Grain*, *Quarry*, *Prairie Fire*, *NeWest Review*, and *Dinosaur Review*. It has also been published in four of Coteau Books' anthologies: *Saskatchewan Gold*, *More Saskatchewan Gold*, *The Old Dance*, and *Prairie Jungle*. She is also a playwright.

Dianne Warren lives in Regina with her family. In addition to writing, she works as a curriculum developer in art education for the Saskatchewan Department of Education.